The Sleepover Club

Have you been invited to all these sleepovers?

Sleepover Club Ponies

by Harriet Castor

An imprint of HarperCollins*Publishers*

The Sleepover Club ® is a
registered trademark of HarperCollins*Publishers* Ltd

First published in Great Britain by Collins in 2002
Collins is an imprint of HarperCollins*Publishers* Ltd
77-85 Fulham Palace Road, Hammersmith,
London, W6 8JB

The HarperCollins website address is
www.**fire**and**water**.com

1 3 5 7 9 8 6 4 2

Text copyright © Harriet Castor 2002

Original series characters, plotlines
and settings © Rose Impey 1997

ISBN 0 00 711884 8

The author asserts the moral right to
be identified as the author of the work.

Printed and bound in England by
Clays Ltd, St Ives plc

Sleepover Kit List

1. Sleeping bag
2. Pillow
3. Pyjamas or a nightdress
4. Slippers
5. Toothbrush, toothpaste, soap etc
6. Towel
7. Teddy
8. A creepy story
9. Food for a midnight feast:
   chocolate, crisps, sweets, biscuits.
   In fact anything you like to eat.
10. Torch
11. Hairbrush
12. Hair things like a bobble or hairband,
    if you need them
13. Clean knickers and socks
14. Change of clothes for the next day
15. Sleepover diary and membership card

CHAPTER ONE

Neeiiigghhh!

Hey, watch out! That's Kenny, doing her mad pony impression again. She'll use us for jumping practice if we don't get out of the way. Quick – let's sit over here for a sec. I haven't seen you for ages and we've got so much to catch up on!

You remember me, don't you? I'm Lyndz (Lyndsey Marianne Collins to give you the full caboodle) and I'm a member of the coolest club in the whole world—

"Universe!"

OK, Frankie! How come she heard that

from half-way across the yard? She must have enormous flappy elephant ears, that girl!

But she's right, the Sleepover Club is the best club in the entire universe, *ever*. And when you hear what we've been up to this time... Well, it's a good job I'm the one who gets to tell you about it, 'cos no one else could give you all the inside goss on *this* story. There's been more drama round here recently than in a whole series of *Brookside*, I reckon! Like that moment when – no, wait, I mustn't spoil it. But I think I got the biggest fright of my life. You'll be on the edge of your seat, I promise!

I'd better start at the beginning, hadn't I, or I'll be gabbling on and you won't have a clue what I'm talking about. For a start – you remember the rest of the Sleepover Club, right? There's Kenny, who nearly landed on top of us just now. She's actually Laura McKenzie to the teachers, but don't call her that or she'll jump on you for real! Kenny's wild about football (weird, huh?), but she's a complete laugh, too. And she is *the* best schemer when it comes to getting back at the M&Ms, our arch-enemies.

Then there's Frankie Thomas. She doesn't really have elephant ears at all, but she does have a seriously LOUD voice. Frankie's always having barmy ideas, and dressing up in even barmier clothes, given half the chance. Just wait till you hear about her latest outfit...

Next comes Miss Felicity Proudlove – that's Fliss for short, of course. She used to be called Sidebotham before her mum married Andy – and you can imagine how much the M&Ms teased her for that. Look, she's over there chatting to Rosie, probably still going on about those hairdos she's mad about. Rosie looks a bit bored, but she's far too nice to say so – typical Rosie!

Rosie's the fifth member of the Sleepover Club. She's ace – and not as crazy as some of the others, which is a relief, I can tell you. Together we have the most awesome time going to sleepovers at each other's houses. We're always making wicked plans for things to do, even if sometimes they go a bit pear-shaped.

And, boy, did things go *super* pear-shaped this time – especially for me! It all started a few weeks ago, on a wet Monday morning. The first bell hadn't even gone yet, but we were in our classroom because of the rain. Everyone was sitting on desks and talking, except for Danny McCloud and Mark Pitt, who were having a scrap in the corner (sad or what?).

Suddenly Frankie burst into the room at a million miles an hour, threw her bag down and boinged up on to the desk beside me.

"Guess what?" she said.

"What?" Fliss, Rosie, Kenny and I all said together.

"My gran came to stay this weekend and she brought me the *coolest* present and it made me have the *coolest* idea and I am just so COOL you should all just gasp."

Kenny did it really well. Her hands shot up to her mouth and her eyes stretched wide, as if Madonna had walked in to take the register.

"Well? What is it?" I said. Frankie had started wriggling out of her coat, in no hurry to spill the beans. She's never happier than when she's got all our attention. I wouldn't put it past her to say she's got a brilliant idea even when she hasn't, just to keep us hanging on.

"What's the idea?" said Rosie.

"What's the present?" said Fliss.

"Quick! Or ve have vays of making you talk!" said Kenny, grabbing Frankie's arm and pushing her sleeve up, pretending she was going to give her a Chinese burn.

Frankie laughed. "It's, like, a bag of treasure," she said.

"*Treasure?*" Kenny's eyes lit up. "Pirate treasure?"

A really strange picture popped into my head of Frankie's gran wearing a black eye patch, with a parrot sitting on her shoulder. It made me giggle.

"Pieces of eight?" said Rosie. "And diamonds and – and gold?"

"Not real treasure. Gran's given up the bank-robbing," said Frankie with a wink. She'd spotted the M&Ms – that's Emma Hughes and Emily Berryman, the snidest snottiest girls in our class – loitering near us.

They're so nosy, they're always listening in to our conversations. When she heard the word 'bank-robbing' Emily Berryman looked really shocked. It was wicked.

Now Frankie leant forward and said more quietly, "It's beads, actually. Gran brought me this big bag of them, and they're amazing. Like jewels. They're all different colours, and some of them have got glitter under the surface so they're really sparkly. Some have tiny patterns painted on them too."

"Wow!" said Fliss.

Kenny groaned. "Yawn, more like," she said. "I thought it was going to be something exciting, Thomas." Kenny's not really into clothes and girlie stuff. She'd wear her Leicester City football top every day if she could.

But Frankie wasn't put off. "And I've had the best idea," she said. "What if we make bracelets for each other? Special bracelets that only members of the Sleepover Club can wear!"

"Pledges of our undying friendship," said Fliss grandly.

"Hey, yeah!" said Rosie. "Like that time with Jewel!" Jewel was a really cool traveller girl we met a while ago. She made us these fab bracelets out of embroidery silk. "And we could always wear them and never take them off," Rosie continued. "Oh, except for school." We're not allowed to wear jewellery, worse luck.

"All the time *except* school, then," I said. "It's a majorly top idea, Frankie. Have you brought the beads in? Can we do it today?"

"I didn't want to risk it with those two lamebrains around," she said, jerking her thumb in the direction of the M&Ms. "And in any case, I thought I'd save them 'cos Mum and Dad said I can have a sleepover."

"Now, that's more like it!" said Kenny, grinning. "This weekend?"

Frankie shook her head. "Gran'll still be here and it'll be too much of a squash, Mum says. How about a week on Saturday? If everyone comes round in the afternoon we could make the bracelets and maybe watch a video, too."

"Hey, we should watch *Friends* – you know,

make it a theme!" said Fliss. "I could bring my tapes." Fliss has every *Friends* video there's ever been. I reckon she must know all the episodes off by heart.

"I'm there – guaranteed!" I said.

"Me too!" said Rosie.

"Can my bracelet be pink?" said Fliss eagerly. "Who's going to make it for me?"

At that moment Mrs Weaver, our teacher, came in. "Settle down, everyone," she shouted, clapping her hands.

"We can sort that out later," Frankie said to Fliss, stepping on to my chair and then clambering over on to her desk.

"Francesca Thomas, this is not a mountaineering class!" shouted Mrs Weaver, sounding cross already.

It was a sign of things to come. Weaver had obviously got out of bed on the wrong side that morning, and the slightest bit of cheek from Danny or chattering at the back had her looking all purse-lipped and thundery. Honestly, it's such a downer when teachers are like that, don't you think? School is bad enough – they could at least try to make it nicer for us by being in a good mood!

She cheered up a bit after the register, though, when she started telling us about a new project she wanted us to work on in our history lessons.

"Who's been to Cuddington library recently?" she asked first.

The M&Ms stuck their hands up. They're such goody-goodies, it's enough to make you sick.

"And did you notice anything new there, Emma?" said Mrs Weaver.

Emma Hughes looked puzzled. "Er... books?" she said.

Behind me, I heard Kenny snort. "Books?" she muttered. "In a library? Omigosh, how shocking!"

Well, that set me off giggling, and once I start I'm a lost cause, my dad says. I was trying to listen to what Mrs Weaver was saying, concentrating on how *un*funny it was.

"I expect they do have some new books, but that's not what I was thinking of, Emma."

15

But all the time I was quaking and shaking, and feeling that if I didn't let these giggles out I was going to...

"Hic!"

Too late! The hiccups had started. I had to put my head on the desk to try and hide. Behind me I could hear Frankie and Kenny spluttering and snorting. The mad thing was, it hadn't even been that funny.

"Lyndsey Collins, whatever is the matter?"

Uh-oh. Frankie always says I should be in the Guinness Book of Records for having the loudest, squeakiest hiccups in the world. Not handy when you're trying to hide.

I lifted my head. "Noth-hic-ing, Mrs Weaver."

"What have I just been saying?"

"Um, about the, hic, library having something new, and it's not new, hic, books..." I was so desperate to laugh, my voice had gone all wobbly.

Mrs Weaver was not amused. "Come and sit over here," she said, pointing to an empty desk right in front of her.

"But Mrs, hic—"

16

"*Now.*" There was no arguing with that tone of voice. It made my hiccups disappear in an instant. I got up and shuffled to the front of the class.

Well, that was the cause of the whole disaster. If I'd been sitting in my usual place I wouldn't have done it. Rosie would have grabbed my arm in the nick of time, or Kenny would've tackled me from behind.

At first everything was OK. Mrs Weaver explained about our projects and I just sat there with a cricked neck, staring up her nose.

"Our projects are going to be about Victorian life," she said, "and the library has an exhibition on at the moment about Leicestershire in Victorian times. We'll go and have a look at it tomorrow – *if* you can all behave yourselves." When she said this she peered down at me. "I want you to get into groups, and each take a different topic for your project. There are six topics, so you may as well stay in the same groups you were in for science yesterday."

This was *way* cool. Yesterday the five of us Sleepover Clubbers had been in a group by

17

ourselves, which doesn't always happen. I turned round and grinned at the others. Frankie gave me a big thumbs-up and Kenny winked.

Mrs Weaver grabbed her marker pen and wrote the six topics on the board. Then she stuck pictures cut from newspapers and magazines next to each one. Next to 'Houses and Homes' there was a grand old house with big windows. Next to 'Sports and Pastimes' there was a footballer, with an old-fashioned haircut and funny big shorts. 'Costume' had a lady in a long dress beside it, probably from one of those Sunday night dramas on the telly, and 'Animals' had a really cute-looking dog. Next to 'Schools' there was a man with enormous whiskers holding a book. He looked twice as grumpy as Mrs Weaver on a bad day - scary!

But 'Transport' was what really caught my attention, because next to that there was a beautiful chestnut pony, with a white stripe down its nose. And, in case you didn't know already, I am just crazy about ponies!

"I really want you to use your imagination with these projects," said Mrs Weaver, turning back to us. "As well as doing written work, you could paint a picture, or make a model or a collage. At the end of term each group will give a presentation to the rest of the class. So, right from the beginning, I want you to be thinking up ways to communicate the things you find out.

"But first we have to allocate the topics. Who's going to do..."

She turned round to look at the board. My bum was on the edge of my seat. There's always such a massive scramble when things get shared out, and I'm wicked at shooting my hand up faster than anyone else. I was ready.

Mrs Weaver pointed to the pony. "...Transport?"

"Yes!" I shouted, my hand blasting into the air like a space rocket.

There was a short silence. I could hear the M&Ms sniggering softly and I looked round.

I'd been the fastest to put my hand up, all right. Because I'd been the *only one*. What's more, Fliss was looking at me like I'd just pulled the head off her Barbie, and Kenny was flapping her hands and shaking her head.

"Excellent," said Mrs Weaver, writing my name down. "Lyndsey's group can do Transport. Now, Sports and Pastimes? Ryan, you were first..."

By now Kenny had flung her hands up in the air and was bashing her head on her desk in despair. Even Rosie was looking at me like I'd made a horrid smell.

Marooned at my front row desk, I felt like the biggest durr-brain on the planet. I knew exactly what I'd done.

"Why, Lyndz? *Why*??"

"Did your brain turn to gloop?"

The bell had gone and we'd all piled out into the playground for break. It had stopped raining, but there were big puddles everywhere. I felt like a puddle myself. The others were giving me a seriously hard time.

"I messed up," I admitted. "I'm sorry, OK?"

"I wanted to do Costume!" Fliss whispered

accusingly. Her eyes were all watery, like she was about to cry.

"You only went and chose THE most boring topic on the list!" wailed Frankie. "What were you thinking of?"

"I – I don't know," I stuttered. "It was that picture, I guess..."

Kenny slapped her forehead. "I might have known it! A picture of a horse and Lyndz loses all control. Not to mention all her brain-power!"

"We could've done loads on horses in Animals," Rosie pointed out.

Kenny groaned, clutching her stomach like she had tummy-ache. "And we could've done stupid horse-racing in Sports..."

Usually with the Sleepover Club, things blow over really quickly. If one of us is feeling a bit cross about something, the others tease them out of it. But not this time. This time it really felt like four against one.

"We know you're horse-mad, Lyndz," said Frankie. "But this is ridiculous."

"*And* you've been spending so much time down at those smelly stables recently,"

21

sniffed Fliss, wrinkling her nose. "You never do anything *we* want to do."

"That's not true!" I said. "I never miss our sleepovers!"

"No, but what about that Saturday when my mum took us to the shopping centre?" said Fliss.

It was true. I had missed that.

"And you never came to see *Shrek* with us!" said Frankie.

"That was *years* ago!"

"What about when I wanted to build that treehouse?" said Kenny.

"But I would've been no use at that," I said.

"It doesn't matter. It's the *principle*," said Fliss haughtily. For a moment she sounded just like her mum. "The Sleepover Club should be the most important thing."

"It is!" I protested.

Fliss shrugged huffily. "Anyone would think you prefer those ponies to your friends!"

"Well, if you're all going to be so completely mean, then maybe I do!" I shouted, and stomped off across the playground. I could feel my cheeks burning

beetroot red, and my eyes w....... ...
like I was about to cry.

What made it a million times wo...
I stomped straight past the M&Ms, ...
doing some silly clapping game. They s....ped
in mid-clap and stood whispering together
with horrible smug smiles on their faces.

So I stalked off round the corner where the
big school bins are kept. It was pongy there,
but at least I was out of sight. I was so cross I
pulled three of the gruesomest faces I could
think of, which usually makes me feel better.

Not this time. I couldn't get over how
unfair it was. Just this morning we'd been
talking about undying friendship and making
those bracelets. And now my four best mates
in the world had turned on me. All because
of some stupid project. Suddenly I was
struck by the most terrible thought:

Was this the end of the Sleepover Club?

CHAPTER TWO

The next lesson was maths, and it was the longest lesson of my entire life.

Does that ever happen to you too? Does time seem to whizz by when you're having a laugh and really drag when you're miserable? To me, two weeks of holiday can go five billion times quicker than two weeks of school. What a bummer.

Well, this maths lesson was exactly like that. I thought the clock had broken, its hands were moving so slowly.

I was back at my old desk, next to Rosie and slap bang in front of Frankie and Kenny. Of

24

course I was ignoring them. But ignoring people is such hard work! You have to concentrate on them all the time, to make sure you don't do something normal by mistake, like look at them or ask to borrow a pen.

Mrs Weaver had written up a load of sums on the board. We were supposed to be working quietly on our own, but I could hear rustling and whispering around me, so I knew the rest of the Sleepover Club were doing something. Saying mean things about me probably, I thought.

But then Rosie slipped a folded piece of paper on to my desk. I opened it, and this is what I saw:

Sorry times a million,
Lyndz!
luv Kenny ❤

We're durr-brains
love from Rosie
xx ❤

Horses are OK really
(just never make me ride one).
Sorry I was horrible.
Love Fliss xxxx ❤

We love you!
Frankie xxx ❤

I was so relieved, it felt like the sun had just come out inside my head. "Oh, guys!" I said, turning round to them with the biggest grin on my face. "I'm sorry too!"

We tried to have a group hug, but it was tricky because Fliss was sitting on the other side of the aisle. And then Mrs Weaver spotted us – "I said no conferring, you girls!" – so we had to turn back to our desks. But I mouthed, "See you at lunch!" and the others all nodded.

It was the best making-up ever. We had a proper hug as soon as the bell went, and then I did high fives with everyone.

"It's a nightmare falling out," said Kenny. "Let's not do it again, all right?"

I nodded, grinning and feeling teary at the same time. "New club resolution."

"Seconded!" said Rosie.

"Thirded!" yelled Frankie.

"You can't say thirded," said Fliss. "But I know what you mean."

While we were waiting in the lunch queue the M&Ms swanned past with their trays already full. They're such greedy guts, they always push to the front.

"Untwisted your knickers yet?" asked the Goblin (that's our name for Emily Berryman) in her weird gruff voice.

"What a shame you've got the *worst* project," smarmed Emma Hughes. "But then, your presentation's bound to be pathetic, so it doesn't really matter, does it?"

"Actually, Transport is the coolest subject," said Kenny, "and anyone with even *half* a brain can see that."

"Not what you were saying to Lyndsey at break," said the Goblin.

"You sneaky little eavesdropper!" gasped Fliss. "You've no right listening in to private conversations!"

The Goblin snorted. "Not worth it when they're as boring as yours."

And before any of us could reply they sailed off with their noses in the air.

"Grrr! What would I give to squash those two toad-faces into a big pile of mushy peas!" growled Kenny.

"We've got to make sure our project is a

27

squillion times better than theirs," said Frankie. "At least!"

"We will," said Rosie firmly, linking arms with me.

Sitting at a different table from the M&Ms, we soon forgot all about them. Kenny kept making farty noises with the ketchup bottle, which made everyone fall about, and Frankie did her impression of Mrs Weaver in a bad mood, which is freakily good. I'd cheered up loads, but there was just one more thing I wanted to say.

"Transport is definitely the coolest subject, of *course*," I began sheepishly, not meaning it at all, "but, guys – you're right that I've missed some Sleepover Club things because of the stables. It won't happen again, I promise."

"It doesn't matter," said Frankie, waggling a chip in the lake of ketchup she'd made on her plate. "We all do other things, like Fliss goes to ballet and Kenny goes to those tedious footie matches. Oof!" Kenny'd grabbed her lunch tray and pretended to boff Frankie over the head with it.

"And anyway," Fliss said, prodding at her salad with her fork, "we don't think all those things we said about the stables, honest."

"Only some of them," said Kenny, with a wicked grin. "The minute you start stinking of horse poo, Collins, I'm outta here!"

You're going to think I'm mad, considering what had happened that day, but when I got home from school all I wanted to do was go to the stables. In three weeks' time there was going to be a gymkhana there – a riding competition with lots of different races and games that you can enter with your pony. I'd played a few gymkhana games before, but I'd never entered a proper competition, so I wanted to do my best.

On my bike I can whizz to the stables in about two minutes, which is dead handy. Today, the moment I got there, I went to see Bramble. She's a lovely bay – brown with a black mane and tail. Of all the ponies at Mrs McAllister's stables, she's my favourite (only don't tell Alfie and Marvel and the others!).

And when you've had a wobbly day at school, there's nothing like having a pair of kind brown eyes to talk to and a lovely warm furry neck to hug.

"Hey, Bramble," I said, stroking her soft nose to say hello. She nuzzled my hand gently. It seemed like she was pleased to see me.

"Hello, Lyndsey!" called Mrs McAllister, who was walking across the yard. She's my riding teacher, as well as being the owner of the stables.

"Hi, Mrs McAllister," I called back. "Can I do some practice today, for the gymkhana?"

Mrs McA looked at her watch and pursed her lips. "Well... give me about half an hour. Then I'll come and watch you do some jumping on. Bramble's had a fair amount of exercise today, so why don't you just give her a gentle warm-up while you're waiting?"

"Great!" I said. "Thanks, Mrs McAllister."

"Glad to see you're so keen, Lyndsey," she said, heading for her office.

"Well, less than three weeks to go now!" I said.

"Two, you mean!" she called, tapping the

poster taped to the office window as she passed. "See you later!" And the office door swung shut behind her.

Two weeks? I frowned, puzzled. But surely the gymkhana was on the 28th? "Wait a sec, Bramble," I whispered, and ran across the yard to have a look at the poster.

**Come to the GYMKHANA
at McAllister's Riding Stables
Sandy Road
Little Wearing
nr. Cuddington
on Saturday 28th January
2pm onwards**

Lots of games and races for teams and individuals.
(Entry forms available from the above address.)

Fun to watch too!

My watch just tells the time. It doesn't have a little date window on it, like Fliss's does, so I'm never the person to ask if you want to know the date (unless it's my birthday!). But for once I could remember Mrs Weaver writing it up on the board this morning: Monday 16th.

Well, I bet you've done the maths already, haven't you? Yep, that's right. Dozy here had been reckoning on nearly three weeks to turn herself into Cuddington's answer to Frankie Dettori when there were less than two. The gymkhana was a week on Saturday!

That was enough of a shock in itself. But the next moment I felt as if Bramble had leapt across the yard and given me the most almighty kick.

"Oh no!" I groaned out loud. "Frankie's sleepover!" She'd said a week on Saturday, hadn't she? And I had promised promised *promised* (cross-my-heart-and-hope-never-to-set-foot-in-a-stirrup-again) not to miss it. What on earth was I going to do?

Through the window I could see Mrs McAllister, the phone pressed to one ear, looking at me weirdly. I was probably grimacing really gruesomely, worse than the

M&Ms with tummy ache. Quickly, I turned round and marched back to Bramble's stable, to tack her up.

Half an hour later, when Mrs McAllister came out to the field and shouted, "How about some jumping on, then, Lyndsey?" I wasn't feeling any better. If anything, I think I was feeling worse. My heart was going ker-*boom* ker-*boom* in my chest, like it was trying to get out, and I kept thinking how desperately I wanted to enter the gymkhana. I *had* to find a way. But how could I, after what I'd said to the others? Especially after the barny we'd had about me preferring ponies to my friends!

It was hard to concentrate. But I needed to – jumping on is really tricky. You see, there are some races where, to be quick enough to stand a chance of winning, you have to get off your pony and get back on again while she's still moving. I'm OK at the flying dismounts (sounds like a circus trick, huh?). It's the vaulting – that is, the getting back on again – that I have problems with, big time.

"Now, try to relax, Lyndsey," said Mrs McAllister. "And remember: watch Bramble's stride. You should jump when the front foot that's *nearest* to you hits the ground."

I nodded. I knew this. It was just easier said than done. And I had quite a few bruises from when I'd messed it up last time.

Trying not to be nervous, I urged Bramble into a canter. I ran alongside, gripping her saddle in one hand and the reins in the other, and watching her feet. I was going to have to jump, swinging my legs out over her back end to land in the saddle.

"Come on Bramble," I whispered breathlessly. "We can do this!"

And then I jumped.

"That was a beauty!" I heard Mrs McAllister call.

I was in the saddle – no bruises. I'd done it!

"Way to go, girl!" I laughed, patting Bramble's neck.

Well, that put me on such a high I thought I'd show off and go straight into a flying dismount. I swung my body forward and my legs back. But one of my feet got caught in its stirrup. My other leg was already swinging over, and I could feel my weight dragging me out of the saddle. The foot that was stuck was twisting now at a really awkward angle, so I couldn't get it out.

It must've all happened in a nanosecond, but to me it felt like some horrid slow-motion dream. Panicking that my foot wasn't going to come free, I let go of the reins and was immediately flung out sideways. The ground swung up towards me with a sickening lurch, and then: *thwack*. Everything stopped dead.

CHAPTER THREE

It took me a moment or two to work out what had happened. I just lay there like a sack of potatoes, with my face in the muddy grass.

"Lyndsey! Lyndsey! Are you all right?" I heard Mrs McAllister's voice right in my ear. She was out of breath; she must've shot across the field like an Olympic sprinter.

I groaned and tried to sit up. But when I pushed on my left hand the most horrible pain shot up my arm. "Owww!" I yelped.

"Don't move yet," said Mrs McAllister. "Where does it hurt?"

"My arm," I gasped. "Left... arm."

Straight away Mrs McAllister sprang into super-efficient emergency gear. First she checked me all over to make sure my arm was the only bit that hurt. Then, ever so gently, she helped me sit up. I was crying by this time, blubbing worse than my little brother Ben (who is the biggest cry-baby in the world, in case you didn't know). I never knew part of me *could* hurt that much. I swear, if your arm felt like mine did right then, you'd have been bawling too!

"All right, Lyndsey. We're going to get you to the hospital," said Mrs McAllister.

"Where's Bramble?" I said, turning my head. My eyes were so full of tears, everything was a splodgy blur.

"She's fine," said Mrs McAllister. "She's away by the fence, nosing about in the grass. Think you can stand?"

I nodded, sniffing loudly. I hoped I hadn't yanked on the reins in my panic and hurt Bramble's mouth. But I couldn't worry about Bramble for long. Getting to Mrs McAllister's Land Rover took all my concentration. My right hand was holding my left arm close to my body to stop it moving, but somehow it still felt as if every step I took gave it a hideous jolt.

Call me crazy, but in the hospital all I could think was: Kenny should be here! Kenny, as you probably know, is dead set on being a doctor when she grows up, like her dad. She just loves all that gruesome medical stuff. If she'd been sitting next to me while I waited in Casualty she would've been bouncing up and down in her chair with excitement and trying to guess what hideous diseases everyone else had.

As it was, I was sandwiched between Mrs McAllister on one side of me and Mum on the other. Miranda, Mrs McA's assistant, had rung my house as soon as we set off for the hospital.

Mum kept saying relieved things like, "Thank goodness you were wearing a hard hat, poppet!"

And Mrs McAllister kept saying apologetic things like, "Believe me, Mrs Collins, I would never let anyone out of the yard without one."

Mrs McAllister was looking quite shaken, actually. I guess it's really rare that anyone hurts themselves at the stables.

They'd given me some majorly strong painkillers, so I was feeling a bit better, though still really sore. It took ages to get everything sorted. They did an X-ray (Kenny would've been in orbit!), which showed that my arm was broken. Then, after another long wait, I had my plaster cast made. *That* felt mega weird.

The cast went from my wrist to just above my elbow, and I was going to have to wear my arm in a sling, the nurse said, to hold it in place. Some slings are quite small, I think, but mine was like an enormous napkin. I felt like an Egyptian mummy!

"How long do I have to wear the cast for?" I asked Mum on the way home.

"Six weeks, the nurse said," Mum replied. We stopped at some traffic lights and she turned to look at me. "Poor pumpkin. You were very brave."

Famous last words! For some reason that just made me burst into tears again. It was probably the shock of it all, Mum said later.

When we got home, Dad came bounding out of the house and opened the car door for me. "But – what's happened to you?" he said, gasping and staring at my plaster cast as if I'd just sprouted an alien growth.

"Da*aad*! You are *such* a bad actor!" I shrieked. "Mum was on the phone to you every five minutes when we were in the hospital. I heard her!"

"Oh. Right you are, then," Dad said, slamming the car door behind me and ruffling my hair in the way that usually really annoys me. Tonight, for some reason, I didn't mind.

Ben and the baby, Spike, were already in bed, but my older brothers Stuart and Tom piled downstairs when they heard us come in. They'd even made a welcome home banner for me out of a couple of old tea towels stapled together.

Before you go thinking they're in any way soppy or nice, though, I should tell you that the banner said:

40

WELCOME HOME, CLUMSY CLOGS!

It was in enormous red letters, so it was pretty embarrassing.

"Mum, can I ring Rosie and Frankie?" I asked. And Kenny and Fliss, I might've added, but I thought I'd stand a better chance if I just started with two. I couldn't believe so much had happened since the end of school, and they didn't even know!

Mum tapped her watch. "It's a bit late for that, don't you think?"

I looked at the clock. It was 10pm! I couldn't believe it. We'd been at the hospital for hours and hours.

"You'll have a surprise for your mates at school tomorrow," said Dad as he kissed me goodnight.

I grinned. I couldn't wait to see their faces.

But d'you know the craziest thing of all? You'll really think I'm stupid, but what with all the fuss and worry at the hospital I hadn't put two and two together. It was only when Mum and Dad had gone to bed, and the house was quiet, and I was lying in the dark

41

beginning to realise that my arm was aching quite a *lot*, actually, that it hit me:

I had to wear my cast for six weeks.

That meant no riding for six weeks.

And no gymkhana.

CHAPTER FOUR

Talk about a major downer. The next morning I felt like I had my own personal black cloud hovering right above my head. It seemed so cruel that I'd put in all that hard work, practising for the gymkhana, and now I wasn't going to be able to take part.

I'd even chosen the spot on my bedroom wall where I was planning to hang my winner's rosette. "Poor Lyndsey," said Dad when I told him at breakfast. "Talk about riding for a fall!" He thought this was brilliantly funny. I scowled into my Shreddies.

My problem with Frankie's sleepover was solved now, of course. I should have been glad. But I couldn't help thinking I would've found some way to do both in the end, if only I'd racked my brains hard enough...

Still, arriving at school cheered me up. I was so chuffed Mum hadn't let me ring my friends the night before. What I would've missed out on!

First there was Kenny, who raced into the playground as usual, then stopped dead in her tracks so that at least three people cannoned into her. It was like that moment in a soppy film when the hero and heroine spot each other for the first time. Except, the way Kenny stared at me, you'd have thought I'd grown three heads.

Then Frankie bounded up and was about to jump on me for a piggyback when Kenny shouted "No!" and launched herself at Frankie in a flying rugby tackle. They ended up sprawled in a heap. I could hear Frankie's voice coming from somewhere under Kenny, saying, "Hey! What was that for, rat-face?"

But before Kenny could answer, Fliss – who'd just that minute turned up with Rosie – shrieked, "Omigosh, Lyndsey! You've hurt your arm!" as if I didn't *know*, which sent Rosie and me into fits of giggles. Fliss stood there saying, "What? What's funny?" which only made us laugh more.

Soon I had the four of them clustered round me, all asking questions at once.

"Did you actually break it, then?" said Frankie, rapping her knuckles on my cast. I nodded.

"Was the bone sticking up through your skin?" asked Kenny, looking hopeful.

"Urgh! I think I'm going to be sick," said Fliss.

"It does sometimes," said Kenny indignantly. She frowned, thinking. "Maybe it was a greenstick fracture."

"What's one of those?" asked Rosie.

"I'm not sure," said Kenny, "but I've heard my dad talking about them."

"Maybe it means your bones have gone mouldy," suggested Frankie.

"Urgh!" That was Fliss again. She was

looking a bit green herself. Then she said, "Don't worry, Lyndz. Do you remember when I broke my ankle?" Do I! Before yesterday I would've said it was one of the most dramatic days of my life. Fliss and Kenny had been trying out some dance moves at one of our sleepovers, when Fliss had come a cropper and ended up with her leg in plaster.

"You'd think a broken bone would look funny when it mended, wouldn't you? But, see..." She waggled her ankle in front of her. "...you can't tell, can you? It hasn't gone fat or anything."

"What do you mean? It's a *balloon*!" shrieked Kenny, and dodged niftily when Fliss tried to kick her. Fliss has delicate little ankles and is dead proud of them.

Thankfully, before this could turn into a full-scale foot fight, the bell rang.

"Been in the wars, Lyndsey?" said Mrs Weaver as we all piled past her into the classroom.

"Riding accident," I said. It sounded good, I thought – grown-up and kind of glamorous.

It was cool, too, when people started asking if they could sign my cast. But Mrs Weaver barked, "Leave that for break-time!" and made everyone go back to their seats.

It turned out that this morning we were going to see the exhibition at Cuddington library Mrs Weaver had told us about. In all the drama with my arm, I'd clean forgotten about our projects.

Two teachers were going with us: Mrs Weaver and Miss Walsh. Before we set off, Weaver gave us one of her behaving-in-public lectures. "Remember that there will be other people besides you looking round the exhibition. And that means I expect very grown-up, considerate behaviour from everybody," she said. "If anyone misbehaves, Mrs Proctor, the head librarian, will never let groups from Cuddington Primary go there again."

"Library ban! Aaargh! A fate worse than death!" whispered Kenny, clasping her hands to her throat and doing some blood-curdling eye-rolling. But then Weaver spotted her and gave her one of her speciality frosty stares.

The library's not far from our school, so we walked. Mrs Weaver made us go two by two, in a crocodile. Rosie had to go in front of me with Regina Hill, but luckily I got paired up with Frankie, and Kenny and Fliss were behind us, so we could all chat on the way.

That was the good bit. The bad bit was that in front of Rosie and Regina were the M&Ms, and they just couldn't resist smirking over their shoulders every two seconds.

"Top riding skills, Collins," said Emma 'the Queen' Hughes at one point. "You must be *really* good."

Beside her, the Goblin was sniggering. "D'you fall off everything you sit on?" she asked. "Even the loo?"

"That's right, kick a girl when she's down!" yelled Frankie. "You are the meanest slimebags in the history of the entire world!"

"Francesca Thomas! If you don't start behaving yourself this instant we shall all turn back and head for school!" boomed Mrs Weaver from the head of the line.

"They started it," muttered Frankie. It was probably a good job Mrs Weaver didn't hear.

"Last night my sis showed me a clip on the internet from *The Lord of the Rings*," said Kenny behind me. "And the goblins are *sooo* gross. They look exactly like Berryman."

"We should've told the director," giggled Rosie. "Think how much money they could've saved on make-up if they'd cast those two!"

That made us all crack up, and gave me an attack of hiccups that lasted the rest of the way to the library.

Cuddington library never used to have exhibitions like this, but a couple of years ago it got a chunk of lottery money, and now there's a brand new gallery built on at the back. *Chimney-sweeps and Crinolines – Leicestershire in the Victorian Era* said the signs as we went in through the big sliding doors.

"I have a feeling," said Frankie gloomily, "that this is going to be a serious yawn."

The first room was full of glass cases. Some of the things in them were quite interesting – ancient lacy gloves, hats with feathers on, old children's toys and a thing called a mangle for squeezing water out of washing – but half the cases seemed to be full of rusty tools.

"We've got junk like this in the shed at home," said Fliss, wrinkling her nose.

"You should take it to the Antiques Roadshow, then," said Rosie. "It could be worth a fortune!"

We hurried on, to a doorway marked *Victorians Come To Life*. From beyond it you could hear singing and laughter and people chattering. "Sounds more fun in here," said Kenny. "Follow me, troops!"

Through the doorway, we found ourselves in a really posh sitting room, like something out of a stately home.

"Cool!" said Rosie, looking about. "It's like Madame Tussaud's!"

"Madame Two-what?" said Kenny.

"That place in London with all the waxworks," said Fliss.

Rosie was right. There was a waxwork of a woman in a long dress by the piano, and another waxwork (a man) sitting playing. Another couple were sitting on an enormous sofa drinking cups of tea, and an older man was standing by a window. They'd put a picture on the other side of the glass to make it look like a real street outside. Hidden somewhere there must have been a tape recorder, because you could hear the woman singing and the piano playing, and a murmur of voices as if the people on the sofa were chatting.

"It's wicked!" I said. "What d'you reckon, Frankie?"

Frankie hadn't said anything since we'd come into the room. Now I noticed she wasn't even beside me – she was still standing by the entrance, staring at her shoes.

I went over to her. "What's up?"

"Look, don't tell the others," she said in a low voice, "and I know I'm a complete wimp – but waxworks give me the screaming abdabs." She glanced up at me briefly. "Can I hang on to you, and not look, and you can kind of lead me through?"

"Seriously?" I couldn't quite believe it. Fearless Frankie, the feistiest girl in the west, scared of a load of dummies? "They're not alive, you know. They're not going to jump out and bite you."

51

Frankie winced. "I'm always thinking they're about to move. Like walking zombies or something."

"You've been watching too much *Buffy*," I laughed.

"Some people are scared of snakes – or wasps, or mice. I'm scared of these, that's all," said Frankie grimly. "Now are you going to help me or aren't you?"

"All right, all right, keep your hair on," I said. Biting my lip to stop myself from grinning, I inched closer to Frankie so she could take hold of my good arm without anyone noticing. Then, as if we didn't have a care in the world, we strolled into the next room.

On the way we passed the M&Ms, and I saw Emily nudge Emma and nod in our direction, whispering something behind her hand. I presumed she was just being snide about my arm again. Later, I wished I'd taken more notice.

I forgot all about the M&Ms as soon as we got into the next room. It was really dark and the air was filled with noise – clangs and crashes. It was supposed to show you what it was like in a Victorian mine, and it was dead realistic.

"This is awesome!" I said. "Frankie, you're really missing out!"

But she wouldn't look up. "Just – keep – going – will you?" she said through gritted teeth, her nails digging painfully into my arm. I should've told her to hold my plaster cast, and I wouldn't have felt a thing!

I guess if you were wobbly about waxworks it must've been pretty spooky. The room was dim and shadowy, and the waxworks weren't grouped in one area, behind a rope barrier – they were dotted about all over the place. To get from one side of the room to the other, you had to weave your way amongst them.

That didn't bother me. But something else caught my attention. "Look – oh, poor thing!" I said, dragging Frankie to where a waxwork of a woman stood next to a model 'pit pony'. "How cruel to make ponies work in a place like this," I said, ignoring Frankie's tugs at my arm. "They must've been so scared."

If I hadn't had my mind filled with those poor pit ponies, I might have spotted that something was up. As it was, I was just about to turn round and set off towards the door when Frankie jerked suddenly as if she'd had an electric shock, and let rip the most blood-curdling scream I have ever heard in my life.

The waxwork next to us, the woman, had moved. Not just moved – it had stuck out an arm and *grabbed Frankie*. For a second everything she'd said about zombies came flooding back and I was pretty panicked too.

Frankie hadn't stopped screaming. It wasn't one "Eek!" and it was all over – she was shrieking, again and again, and making a dash for the exit, pushing and shoving in her panic to get out. She even managed to knock over one of the waxworks, which toppled against another one, and sent them both head-first into a wagon of coal.

Everyone else in the room – not sure if Godzilla was about to burst in, or if one of the waxworks had a bomb under its hat – started jostling around, some people heading for the exit, others back the way they'd come and some people just milling about, asking each other what'd happened.

Meanwhile, standing right where Frankie had left me, I saw something no one else spotted: a person emerging from behind the waxwork that'd 'moved'. Even in the dim light I could see a really slimy smirk spread all over her face.

"What happened? Where's Frankie?" said Kenny, suddenly right at my elbow.

Before I could reply, an announcement came over the tannoy, like at the supermarket. Except instead of, "Supervisor to checkout three, please," it said, "Cuddington Primary group, go to the exit immediately."

"Uh-oh," said Kenny. "Weaver's pulled the plug. Come on."

We had to assemble outside in the car park, where Miss Walsh was standing, her face as sour as if she'd been sucking a whole bag of lemons.

"Don't you *dare* make a noise!" she hissed, as we shuffled into a group and waited for Mrs Weaver to arrive. Frankie had been standing beside Miss Walsh, digging her toe into the gravel, but now she came and joined the rest of us. We eyed each other, but didn't say a thing.

At last Mrs Weaver emerged through the sliding doors, looking flushed, with one of the librarians walking beside her. I heard Mrs Weaver say, "Once again, I am *so* sorry," to the librarian. Then she stalked over to us.

"I expected better from you," was all she said, her eyes raking round the group. And then we set off in a straggly line back to school.

"Why do they always shout at all of us?" said Kenny at break, slumping on the bench. We'd had a good fifteen minutes of Mrs Weaver blasting us, telling us how she and Miss Walsh had "never been so embarrassed in their entire lives" – all the usual teacher guff. "No offence to Frankie, but it was a one-girl stampede. Personally, I was behaving like a super-swotty goody two-shoes..."

"I saw you with one of the waxworks!" said Rosie. "You were sticking a pencil up its nose!"

"That was a serious experiment!" said Kenny. Then she grinned. "Kind of."

"I wonder if Frankie's OK," said Fliss. Right this minute Frankie was inside the office of Mrs Poole, our headteacher.

"Oh, she'll be fine," said Kenny confidently. "You know Pooley – she's way softer than Mrs Weaver. She'll probably tell Frankie to *try* not to do it again and then she'll crack open a packet of Hob-nobs. Talk of the devil..."

"Hey guys!" It was Frankie, bombing towards us across the playground.

"So what happened?" asked Fliss. "Have you got a million detentions?"

Frankie shook her head happily, still getting her breath back. "Pooley tried to be really strict," she said at last, "but when I explained that I hadn't been messing around – that the waxwork really *had* moved – she turned all sympathetic, and said it would've scared her too. Apparently she knows the head librarian and she's going to have a word. She reckons that if exhibitions have moving parts they should *warn* you at the

57

beginning. She said if someone with a dodgy heart had a shock like that it could make them keel over."

"Good for Pooley," said Kenny.

"Except she'll find out from the librarian that the waxwork didn't move," I said.

"It did!" insisted Frankie. "It grabbed me! Though probably by chance, Mrs Poole said – it couldn't really have been programmed to do that." She frowned. "Blimey, Lyndz, why don't you believe me?"

"I do believe you," I said. "But I saw something. After you'd gone."

I'd been dying for a chance to tell them ever since the bell rang. Now I had everyone's attention. Even Kenny sat up straight and stared at me.

"Someone was hiding behind the waxwork," I said. "*They* grabbed you. On purpose."

"You saw them? Who was it?" Frankie was looking at me in astonishment. "Who, Lyndz? Who?"

CHAPTER FIVE

Who grabbed Frankie? I bet you've got a pretty good idea, haven't you, and you weren't even there! You could narrow it down to two, anyhow: our two worst enemies, the M&Ms.

I took a deep breath. "Emma Hughes," I said.

I think Frankie'd had a hunch too, because she didn't look shocked – she just looked furious. "What I'd like to do to that twisted, snotty, fat-bottomed *fartbrain*!" she snarled.

"I saw her when Mrs Weaver was bawling us out," said Rosie. "She had the slimiest 'I'm-so-perfect' look on her face. Ugh! Why does she always get away with it?"

"She doesn't – not this time," said Kenny darkly. "Nobody plays a trick like that on the Sleepover Club without *paying* for it!"

As you can imagine, we spent the whole of the rest of break complaining about the M&Ms. We could spend years on that subject, I reckon!

"You know what I heard them saying to Alana?" said Rosie. "That she couldn't be their friend because she doesn't wear the right clothes at the weekends."

"Yeah, like *they're* such style queens," said Fliss. "Not!"

"They're just the pits," declared Frankie. "And we have *so* got to get them back for setting me up like that."

There was silence while we all tried to think how.

"We should kung fu them," suggested Kenny, "like in *Crouching Tiger, Hidden Dragon*." We'd all seen that video round at Rosie's at our last sleepover. Now Kenny turned into her own version of a kung fu whirlwind, her arms chopping and her legs flailing – until she tripped over one of her big feet and went sprawling on the tarmac.

"Ow." She sat up, rubbing her knee. "OK. Maybe not. I think it takes a bit of practice."

Then the bell rang. "We'll think of something," I whispered to Frankie as we lined up. "It'll be the best revenge plan ever. No fear."

I have to admit, though, I hadn't had a single idea by the end of school. And when I got home, the whole Frankie revenge drama flew clean out of my head when I saw a large white envelope waiting for me on the kitchen table.

Don't you just love getting post? I grabbed the envelope and tore it open without even waiting to take my coat off. Inside was a card, with a picture of a girl riding a beautiful black pony on the front. Inside it said:

To a very promising – and brave! – rider,
Wishing you a speedy recovery
Mrs McAllister
Miranda

I read it over three times. Mrs McAllister had never said I was "very promising" before. This almost made breaking my arm worthwhile!

"Can I go to the stables?" I said to Mum.

"What, now?" Mum laughed. "You can't keep away from that place for five minutes, can you?"

"I'll go on my bike."

"Not with your arm like that." Mum checked her watch. "I promised I'd take some books round to Mrs Clark, so I suppose I could drop you on my way and pick you up on the way back. You wouldn't have very long there..."

"That's OK. I just want to thank Mrs McAllister for the card."

"All right, then. Give me fifteen minutes."

When I got to the stables, I found preparations for the gymkhana in full swing. I must admit, it made my heart sink. Why had I had my accident *now*?

I poked my head round the office door, and found Miranda sewing flags. I thanked her for the card.

"You're welcome— ouch!" She stuck her finger in her mouth. "I tell you, if I'd known working at a stables involved so much sewing I'm not sure I would've taken the job."

"Sorry I can't help," I said, waggling my plaster arm.

Miranda winked. "You're well out of it," she said. "Shame about missing the gymkhana, though. You were coming on so well."

The next moment Mrs McAllister hurried past me and picked up the phone.

"I got your card. It's lovely!" I said as she flipped through the phone book and started to dial.

Mrs McAllister flashed me a smile. "Don't you worry, Lyndsey," she said. "We'll soon have you riding again."

I backed out of the office. They were clearly too busy to chat. Instead I walked over to one of the fields that Mrs McAllister rents from Mr Brocklehurst's farm next door. As well as games at the gymkhana, there was going to be a small course of jumps. They'd been set up in this field.

One of the jumps was made out of tyres threaded on to a pole, another was made of a pile of straw bales. Then there were wooden poles painted with bright red and white stripes, some fitted on to stands and some on to plastic blocks.

I've only had a go at jumping once or twice. Now I stood and watched one of the bigger girls, Lisa Bentham, practising on a pony called Trojan. Have you ever seen show jumping? What's so awesome about it is how beautiful the horses look when they leap over the fences – the way their forelegs tuck up and their backs arch... For a split second it's like they can fly.

The weird thing today, though, was that every time Trojan took off, my stomach lurched. In my mind's eye I could see Lisa tumbling out of the saddle and landing – *splat* – in the grass. How weird is that? I knew she wasn't actually going to fall off – she's really good at jumping and Trojan is dead reliable. But still I kept getting this strange feeling.

I shook my head and turned away. A moment later I'd forgotten all about it. I was too busy looking out for Mum's car and chatting to Miranda, who'd come out into the yard. Maybe I should've been more worried. I'd thought that breaking my arm was the worst thing that could happen to me. Little did I know that my riding troubles were only just beginning...

The next day, I didn't tell anyone at school what'd happened at the stables. I couldn't tell them how down I felt about missing the gymkhana – and besides, there was plenty to take my mind off it. For one thing, Kenny was acting strangely.

"Is she up to something, d'you reckon?" whispered Rosie in the middle of English.

"No idea. Why?" I said.

Rosie shrugged. "She's not usually this... *helpful*, that's all."

It was true. A minute ago, when Mrs Weaver had asked for a volunteer to collect in our science books, Kenny had shouted, "Me!" like the keenest cheerleader ever. Right at this moment she was heading our way, a growing pile of exercise books under her chin.

I held out my book to Kenny, eyeing her suspiciously. She replied with a large wink.

"*Definitely* up to something," I muttered. But as Kenny plonked the books on Mrs Weaver's desk and came back to her seat, I couldn't work out what it might be.

"What're you aiming for?" asked Frankie ten minutes later when we were out in the playground. "Nature table monitor?"

"Get real," Kenny snorted. "Do I look like teacher's pet material? It's part of my cunning plan." Glancing round to check no one was watching, she pulled a piece of paper out from under her jumper and unfolded it. "See!"

"What's that?"

"It was tucked inside Emily Berryman's exercise book."

I grabbed it and examined it carefully. I was expecting to see something top secret. No such luck. It was just some notes from the lesson we'd done on food and digestion.

"Science notes?" I said. "So?"

Kenny grinned. "Top quality McKenzie plan."

"Are you going to tell us or what?"

"I don't want to spoil the surprise. It'll be wicked."

"OK, mystery queen, have it your own way," said Frankie. "See if we care!"

But we did care, of course. We were seething with curiosity.

In the next lesson, we were due to start work on our projects. That meant the Sleepover Club sitting round a desk, with a pile of books from the school library in the middle. Frankie got out her new best pen. It had neon pink feathers stuck on the end, which wafted as she wrote.

"So," she began, underlining the word 'Project' at the top of a clean sheet of paper. "Any ideas?"

"I want to do something about the mines," I said. "And how awful it was to make ponies work in those places."

"Never mind the ponies, what about the people?" said Kenny. "They had to crawl through tunnels, dragging carts, or hacking at the coal all day every day. How hideous is that?"

"Eeuch! Why do we have to think about the miserable stuff?" said Fliss. "I want to do something about the posh houses and those ladies in beautiful dresses..."

"Wait up a second," interrupted Frankie. "We've already got our subject, remember? Transport. So mines are out, and swanky dresses are out too, I'm afraid."

In the disappointed silence that followed, all my guilty feelings came flooding back.

But Frankie sounded cheerful. "Let's have a campaign plan. We need to know what we're looking for in these books, right?" We nodded. "So..." she said, her pen poised, "what are exciting things to do with transport?"

"Racing cars!" said Kenny.

"Spaceships!" said Rosie.

"Enormous limousines, like film stars travel in," suggested Fliss.

"Hmm," said Frankie, tapping her pen on her cheek. "I'm not sure how many of those things were around in Victorian times."

A few moments later, we had a different list. "Right," said Frankie, scanning down it.

"You look at trains, Kenny, and I'll see if I can find anything on trams. Rosie and Fliss, you look for books on bicycles and carriages and things. And of course, Lyndz, you're horses."

I found a chapter in a book called *Working Horses*, and had my nose well stuck into it when I heard Fliss say, "Kenny, what *are* you doing?"

"Oh, just practising my handwriting," Kenny said breezily. A few moments later she stood up saying she wanted to look for another book, and headed for the shelves on the far wall. On her way back, I saw her slip a piece of paper under the edge of Ryan Scott's pencil case, with half of it left peeking out so he'd be sure to spot it.

It took Ryan a few minutes to notice the paper. But when he did, he read it and snorted with laughter. Then he turned round and looked at someone. It was odd. I could've sworn he looked straight at the M&Ms.

"I just have to go to the staff room for a moment," said Mrs Weaver. "Carry on working, everyone. *Quietly.*"

By this time Danny McCloud, who sits next to Ryan, was desperate to know what the note said. He grabbed it off Ryan and read it quickly, and then started making terrible strangulated sicky noises and pulling really disgusting faces.

This, of course, drew the attention of half the rest of the class. Soon the note was travelling round at lightning speed, causing muffled squeaks and snorts.

"Kenny, what on earth does it say?"

"It says, 'Emma H. fancies Fog-brain'," said Kenny. 'Fog-brain' is the class nickname for Danny McCloud (cloud – fog, get it?). "But the best thing is, it says it *in the Goblin's writing*."

"How come?" How could Kenny have made Emily write what she wanted? Then it struck me. "Duh! All that writing practising you were doing!"

"I nicked that page of notes so I could copy how she writes, see?" said Kenny, grinning from ear to ear at her achievement. "Am I or am I not a total genius?"

"Total!" laughed Rosie.

"Way to go, girl!" said Frankie.

I flapped my hands. "Shh! Don't look too pleased or they'll work out who did it."

Immediately, Kenny wiped the smile off her face and got back to her book, sneaking glances every so often from under her hair.

For now the M&Ms didn't have a clue what was going on. But they would find out soon. I watched the progress of the note round the room. Soon it reached us.

"Look like you don't know what it says!" instructed Frankie, and we all huddled round it, nudging each other and giggling.

At long last I saw Regina Hill push the note on to Emily Berryman's desk.

"Nooo!" breathed Kenny, watching. "Don't give it to Emily! She'll hide it. Oh, botheration."

The Goblin unfolded it. All of a sudden she went deathly pale and then, the next moment, bright red. She turned the note over and back again, looking confused. Then Emma Hughes leant across, and asked what it was. Emily tried to hide the note, and there was a short hissed argument. Then Emma grabbed the note and read it.

71

"What?" we heard her splutter. "How *could* you?"

"I didn't write it," Emily protested.

"Don't even try to pretend," snapped Emma. "It's your writing! Look – it's got those pathetic little hearts you draw on your 'i's!" Emma waved the note under Emily's nose. Then she hissed, "I told you it was a *secret*."

"Omigosh!" gasped Kenny, her eyes widening. "Don't tell me she really does fancy Danny!"

Well, it turned into the biggest row between the M&Ms any of us had ever seen. Emma told Emily she was a "traitor" and "the sneakiest blabbermouth ever", while Emily shouted back that Emma was fat and spotty and she'd never liked her anyway. Meanwhile, half the class clapped and cheered, while the other half chanted, "Emma fancies Daa-nny! Emma fancies Daa-nny!"

None of us noticed when Mrs Weaver walked back into the room.

"RIGHT!" she thundered, slamming a pile

of books on to her desk. "I've had just about ENOUGH of this class!"

"Oh no," groaned Kenny. "Now we're *really* for it."

CHAPTER SIX

I guess, after all the stuff at the library, Mrs Weaver was never going to let us off lightly.

"But that was harsh," said Frankie later that afternoon, when we were in the cloakroom getting ready to go home. "I mean, detention! For the entire lunchbreak! Bummer or what?"

"And why did she have to make us write out spellings?" said Rosie. "Torture!"

"But hey," whispered Kenny, flapping her coat to get the sleeve the right way out. "You have to admit – it was worth it, right?"

"Totally," nodded Frankie. Fliss, who hates getting into trouble with the teachers more than she hates Alien Ant Farm (and that's a *lot*), didn't look so sure.

For my part, I was well pleased that the Sleepover Club – thanks to Captain Kenny – had got its super-cool revenge on the M&Ms. On the way home, though, it occurred to me: in all the excitement, we'd hardly made any progress on our projects. I was prepared to bet my best riding boots that the M&Ms hadn't got very far either, considering how they still weren't talking to each other. But I didn't want to take any chances.

That night I made a decision. I, Lyndsey Collins, had dumped the worst, most boring project topic on my friends. So *I* was going to be the one to get us out of the mess. Yes – I was going to have a mega-fantastic idea.

It turned out that that was the easy bit. Deciding to have a great idea is one thing. Actually *having* one... well, I spent most of the next week discovering that that's something else entirely.

At least, now that I wasn't heading off to the stables most days after school, I had plenty of time to think about it. I scoured our house for books that might help. Dad, being an Art teacher, had a couple about Victorian paintings, but that was it.

"Tom?" I poked my head round my brother's door. "Got any books on the Victorians?"

"You're joking, aren't you?" His eyes were glued to his computer screen. He didn't even turn his head. Brothers! Useless, huh?

I tried sitting and *thinking*, but my baby brother Spike was having a screaming fit and Ben was grizzling, just to join in, so it was no use at all.

"Lyndsey, if you've got nothing to do..." began Mum.

I know that hassled look of hers. She was about to give me a heap of washing or ironing or cleaning or something equally awful, so I said, "I'm thinking, actually. It's my homework," and dashed out into the garden.

I stumped across to my dad's workshop (really more like a shed), and found him inside, up to his elbows in clay, making another of his weird lumpy pots.

He didn't seem to mind me being there, so I fiddled around for a while, looking at his paints and brushes. There were some enormous cardboard boxes left over from when he'd bought a new lawnmower and a DIY workbench. I even climbed into one of them and sat in it for a while. And that's when I had it: my brilliant idea.

Do you ever forget what day it is? The next morning, when I hadn't properly woken up yet and my brain was still fuzzy with sleep, I was sure it was a school day.

And then I remembered it was Saturday – which was cool.

But then I remembered it was the day of the gymkhana – which was not cool.

And *then* I remembered it was also the day of Frankie's sleepover. Which was majorly, fantastically awesome. And that I'd got my fab idea to tell everyone about. Which was even better.

Honestly, before I even got out of bed, my mood had gone up and down like a yo-yo!

Mum drove me to Frankie's after lunch. We passed a load of horseboxes coming the other way, heading for McAllister's stables. *That* was a nightmare – just thinking about Bramble and how I could have been tacking her up for the gymkhana right now made my chin go all trembly.

But as soon as Frankie flung open her front door, saw the monster bag of marshmallows I was clutching, and squealed, "Here she is! The marshmallow queen! Are we glad to see *you*!", I felt a load better. Sleepovers *rule*, as Kenny would say!

In the sitting room, I found Kenny, Rosie and Fliss sprawled on the carpet. Fliss had her bag open and was unpacking enough *Friends* videos for about nine sleepovers.

"We don't have to watch them *all*," she said, stacking Series 2 on top of Series 1. "But I thought we should have a choice."

"Well, I reckon we've got enough sweets to get us through a TV marathon," said Rosie. It was true. There was a major heap of Minstrels, Liquorice All-Sorts, Jelly Babies and Toffee Popcorn, even without my marshmallows.

"*And* we've got to make the bracelets!" said Frankie, holding up a big clear plastic bag that sparkled and twinkled in the light. The beads were loads of different colours – deep reds and purples and blues, gold and silver (Frankie's fave colour – no wonder she was so pleased), plus delicate pinks and apple greens and lilacs.

"Wow! They are beautiful!" breathed Fliss. Even Kenny looked impressed.

"Before we start the fun stuff," I said, "can I tell you something?"

Instantly my friends looked at me eagerly. "Is it juicy gossip?" asked Frankie.

"'Fraid not," I said. "It's just that I've had an idea for our presentation."

"Glad somebody has!" said Kenny. "'cos I was getting nowhere."

"Me neither," said Rosie. "Sock it to us, Lyndz."

"Well..." Suddenly, with them all looking at me, I wondered whether it was such a good idea after all. But I ploughed on. "...My dad's got these giant bits of cardboard, you see, so I thought we could make big cardboard cut-outs of things. Like a train, and a horse, and one of those old-fashioned bicycles – you, know, the really tall ones..."

"Penny farthings," said Frankie.

"That's it." I nodded. "And one of us could stand on a chair and hold the picture below them to make it look like they're riding the bike. Someone at the back could hold up the train, and make it go along. And then instead of just giving speeches or whatever we were going to do, we could make it into a little scene. Say, a posh lady comes along in a carriage and meets the man on the bicycle, and they have a chat about these new things called trains..."

"Bagsy I'm the posh lady!" said Fliss. "I've got a long dress and everything!"

Frankie gasped. "You know what the best thing would be?" she said. "Two of us should be the horse that's pulling the carriage – the front end and the back end, like in a Christmas panto! It'd be hilarious!"

"You and me!" yelled Kenny, grabbing Frankie and scrambling to her feet. Frankie bent over, and held Kenny round the waist.

Kenny put her hands up as ears and pawed the ground with her foot, and they set off galloping round the room.

Suddenly Frankie broke away, holding her nose. "Hey, Kenny, did you parp?"

"Baked beans for lunch – sorry," said Kenny sheepishly while the rest of us roared with laughter.

"You're *definitely* the back end next time," said Frankie, flopping down on the carpet.

"That is a seriously cool idea, Lyndz," said Rosie.

"It's top," agreed Kenny. "But where are we going to get a horse costume?"

"Make it?" I suggested. "Brown tights, brown T-shirts – we could get some wool for the tail."

"And we could make a mask for the face," added Rosie.

"Wicked," said Kenny. "Chuck us the popcorn, someone – I've worked up an appetite here."

I grabbed the bag and tossed it to Kenny. I was so chuffed that my friends liked my idea, I felt like boogying round the room!

As it turned out, a chance for that came soon enough. Frankie brought in some juice and we all slurped and munched our way through two episodes of *Friends*. We made a rule that every time the theme music came on, we had to dance around like they do in the fountain at the beginning.

"I'll be there for yoooouuu!" we sang at the tops of our voices.

After that we were pretty exhausted (not to mention a bit queasy from the sweets-and-juice-and-bopping combination), so Frankie fetched needles and thread and we got down to making the bracelets. I was doing one for Kenny. "Can you make it in Leicester City colours?" she asked.

"You'll be lucky to have any colours at this rate," I said. It was pretty tricky with my arm in plaster. In the end, Rosie had to do half of it for me.

After that we had the ceremonial trying-on of the bracelets. Kenny had made Frankie's too small, but Rosie – who has smaller hands – offered to swap, so it was fine. Then we plunged into the marshmallows and gorged ourselves on pink and white squish until it was time to get into our pyjamas.

"Look!" giggled Kenny, who'd shut her eyes and was somehow managing to grip a marshmallow in each eye socket. "I am the marshmallow monster! Aaarrrgh!"

If it hadn't been so hilarious it would've been dead scary. We laughed so much that I got a major attack of the hiccups and Rosie's Coke came out of her nose.

"Ach! That hurts!" she said, shaking her head.

At that moment Frankie's dad put his head round the door. "Er... I'm not even going to ask," he said, looking round at the mess and our flushed faces. "Teeth cleaning then lights out, you rowdy rabble!"

Soon we were snuggled down in our sleeping bags. We switched on our torches and talked for a while about how cool it'd be if we all lived just across the hall from one another, like they do in *Friends*. Then Frankie's mum insisted it was torches-off time. It was hard to get comfy with my plaster cast, and I thought I was never going to get to sleep. As I lay there blinking into the dark, I suddenly realised I'd hardly thought about the gymkhana all day. Now it was over. And I started wondering who had winner's rosettes on their bedroom wall tonight...

"Lyndsey, there you are!" said Mrs McAllister, striding towards me across the yard. "I've been looking all over for you. It's your turn on the jumps course. Now! Hurry, hurry!"

Bramble was beside me, all tacked up and ready to go. The yard was crowded with riders and ponies, and ahead I could see lots of people milling around the edges of the field. I led Bramble across the yard. Then I put my foot in the stirrup and quickly swung myself up into the saddle.

It was only then that a cold feeling crept over me. The field, I could see, was dotted with fences made out of wooden poles, straw bales and old tyres. "Bramble!" I whispered. "This can't be right. We're not entered in the jumps, are we?"

84

All about me, unfamiliar faces were staring. "But I've never jumped proper fences," I wanted to say. I hadn't even walked round the course. What order were you supposed to take the jumps in? How on earth were we going to do it?

"Number five: Lyndsey Collins," came the voice over the tannoy.

I had to say something. I had to tell them that I couldn't do it. But Bramble seemed to have other ideas. She was trotting forward of her own accord.

What do I know about jumping? I thought desperately. Approach in a straight line. Lean forward from the hips – but not too soon. Keep your back straight... oh help!

We were coming up to the first jump. Somehow it had grown. Instead of a few bales of straw I saw a looming green bank, like something out of the Grand National. We didn't have a hope.

But Bramble was heading straight for it. "Wait, Bramble! Whoa!" I kept saying, but somehow the reins had slipped from my hands and there was nothing I could do. I grabbed hold of her mane. Now she was taking off, and jumping higher and higher...

... and suddenly I was out of the saddle and falling. The world was spinning around me in a sickening blur. I didn't know where the ground was, or how soon I would hit it.

And, in the distance, I heard Mrs McAllister screaming, "Lyndsey, Lyndsey! No!"

CHAPTER
SEVEN

"Lyndz. *Lyndz!* It's OK. Wake up!"

Suddenly, I felt someone shaking me. I groaned, and opened my eyes to find Fliss leaning over me, peering at me in bleary concern. Rosie, Frankie and Kenny were sitting up in their sleeping bags, their hair muzzed up from sleep.

"Were you having a nightmare?" asked Rosie.

"Your breathing went really weird," said Fliss. "Kind of whimpery. It was freaky."

I rubbed my face. "I – I was falling..." I stammered.

"Falling?" echoed Kenny, rubbing her eyes.

"Were you dreaming about riding?" asked Rosie gently. "About the accident?"

I nodded, remembering. Then I shivered. "It was horrible."

"Poor Lyndz," said Fliss, putting her arm round me.

"This calls for emergency treats," declared Frankie. She wriggled out of her sleeping bag. "Will hot chocolate do?"

"That'd be great," I said.

"Er, Frankie..." said Kenny, putting on a weak and trembly voice. "I think I had a nightmare too."

"And me," giggled Rosie.

"OK, OK, I get it." Frankie grinned. "Hot chocolate all round." A few minutes later she came back carrying a tray crowded with mugs of steaming cocoa. She'd even found some leftover marshmallows to float in the top.

"Feeling any better?" she asked, handing me a mug.

My smile felt a bit wobbly, but I nodded. "Miles. Thanks."

Rosie blew on her cocoa to cool it. "Are you missing riding a lot, Lyndz?" she said.

I couldn't tell them about today's gymkhana. After that argument we'd had at school, I couldn't even tell them how I really felt. I wanted to say "desperately". But instead I shrugged and said, "A bit, I guess. I'm not really thinking about it to be honest – except in my sleep. There's enough going on with you guys!"

And there *was* enough going on over the next few weeks. Though it didn't stop me missing riding, it certainly kept me busy! We had to design the pictures that we were going to turn into cardboard cut-outs – Dad said he'd help me with the actual cutting. Then the cut-outs were going to need painting. There were our costumes to sort out, too. And on top of all that, we had to decide what we were going to talk about – "write the script of the show!" as Frankie kept saying. *That* ended up involving loads of head-scratching and pencil-chewing.

"I can't do a speech if I'm the back end of the horse," said Kenny in class one day when we were having another project meeting. "Whoever heard of a horse with a talking bottom?"

Rosie giggled. "But Mrs Weaver won't like that," she said. "She'll think you've done no work."

"Suits me!" grinned Kenny.

"Not so fast, lazybones," Frankie jumped in. "Whatever we're going to say we should share."

Kenny blew a raspberry. "Spoilsport. Anyway, we've got to make it short and snappy or there'll be no time for our dance routine."

"What dance routine?" I said. "You're joking, right?"

"No way!" Kenny laughed. "You can't have a panto horse without a little comedy dancing, can you?"

Frankie nudged me. "Kenny and I have been practising. We'll give you a free demo at break if you like."

Though I didn't say anything, I wasn't at

all sure about the idea of a dance routine. Mrs Weaver had talked about "imaginative presentation", but I was pretty convinced that meant getting historical facts across without boring everyone to tears, not just prancing about.

At break Frankie led the way to the Sleepover Club's venue for top secret meetings: the corner of the playground nearest the bins where no one else goes (and if you're wondering why, you should come and catch the whiff sometime). "I know it's stinky," said Frankie when Fliss complained, "but we don't want anyone nicking our toptastic ideas, do we?"

Then Kenny bent over and grabbed Frankie round the waist. "Ready?" she said. "One, two, three..."

There were kicks, stamps and shimmies. Frankie tossed her imaginary mane and Kenny wiggled her bum. But soon Kenny was out of step with Frankie, doing her kicks in the wrong places, and falling over her own feet. It was just about the most hilarious thing I'd ever seen.

"Stop!" I gasped, as Rosie and I held on to each other, laughing fit to burst. "You'll make me, hic, wet myself!"

Suddenly we heard Fliss gasp. She was our official look-out, keeping watch round the corner of the gym block in case anyone tried to spy on us. Instantly we all stopped laughing. Frankie said, "What? What is it?"

Fliss didn't turn her head, but her arm reached back and beckoned us. "You have *got* to see this..." she said.

We squashed up next to her, poking our heads round the wall.

The most amazing sight swung into view.

It was Emma Hughes and Danny McCloud. Holding hands.

"Oh – my – gosh," whispered Frankie. "Gross or *what*?"

Ducking back behind the wall, we stared at one another in astonishment.

"*Bleurgh!*"

Then Kenny slapped a hand to her forehead. "What have I done?" she wailed. "This is all my fault! It's hideous! It's unnatural!"

When the bell rang and we piled back into the classroom, we noticed that the Queen and the Goblin were talking to one another again. More than that – it looked as if they were better friends than ever.

"Emma probably thinks Emily helped get her and her *darling* Danny together," whispered Frankie.

"It turns my stomach just thinking about it," said Fliss.

"But you know the good thing?" said Kenny. "I reckon Emma will spend so much time mooning over Fog-brain she won't give a thought to their lousy project. And the Oscar for best presentation will go to... us!"

Our class was going to give the presentations on the last day before half-term. The rest of the Sleepover Club were counting the days till then. But I was counting the days till something else. The week before half-term, my plaster cast was due to come off, and on the Saturday I was going to have my first riding lesson.

I can't even begin to tell you how excited I was. Riding was the thing I loved doing most in the world and I hadn't been able to do it for six whole weeks. And each one of those six weeks had felt like a year, just about.

When the day my cast was due to come off finally arrived, I was so jittery I couldn't sit still. My eldest brother Stuart drove me to the hospital, and I could tell I was getting up his nose with my fidgeting, but I just couldn't help it.

"Will it hurt?" I asked, winding my window a centimetre up and then a centimetre down – up and down, up and down.

"Hideously," said Stuart. "They do it with a great big saw, and if it gets stuck they have to chop your whole arm off."

"No!" I looked at him, aghast.

"Of course not, dumbo!" he grinned at me in the driver's mirror. "You are so easy to tease!"

I stuck out my tongue. "And you are so mean!"

After that I didn't want to let him see I was scared when they brought out the electric whizzy thing and started cutting through the plaster. In a way it was better, pretending to be brave. With Mum I'd probably have been bawling my eyes out. But I couldn't have been hiding my nerves that well, because the nurse smiled at me and said, "Don't worry. I've done this before."

When the cast finally snapped off it was such an ace feeling. My skin underneath had been getting majorly itchy – and not being able to scratch has to be *the* most frustrating thing in the world. "Hello arm," I said. It looked pale and bruised and strange.

"That's it, I knew it," laughed Stuart. "Talking to your own arm! You're actually bonkers, aren't you?"

By Saturday I'd just about got used to having two normal arms again – in the nick of time for my riding lesson.

"Take care at the stables, though, won't you, love?" said Mum at breakfast time, as she tried to spoon baby food into Spike's ear (he'd turned his head and she hadn't noticed yet). "Your arm'll be a bit weak for a while."

I nodded and carried on squashing my

Weetabix into a soggy mound. My tummy was full of excited butterflies, and all I could think about was what it would be like to hold Bramble's reins again. I hoped she would be pleased to see me – because I was going to be on cloud nine seeing her!

"Happy day, Lyndsey!" called Mrs McAllister across the yard as I jumped out of Dad's car and slammed the door.

I ran straight to Bramble's stall. She nodded her head when she saw me, and didn't seem to mind when I pressed my face against her neck and drank in her warm, clean smell.

"I have missed you," I whispered as I stroked her nose. "More than anything, ever."

Later, when Bramble was tacked up and ready, Mrs McAllister helped me fasten the chin strap of my riding helmet. Then she helped me up into the saddle, so I wouldn't put too much strain on my left arm.

"Now take it gently, Lyndsey," she said. "Give yourself time to get used to Bramble again."

I hardly heard her. Bramble was standing quite still, being really sweet and patient, waiting for me to tell her to walk on. But I felt totally weird – as if I was in a bubble, cut off from the scene around me. The colour of Mrs McAllister's coat, the stable doors, even the reins in my hand, looked too bright and my stomach was churning. Suddenly I knew I was either going to be sick or faint – or maybe both.

"I – I have to get down," I said.

"Steady, there. You're all right." Mrs McAllister patted my leg.

"No, I have to get down," I insisted. "*Now*."

Mrs McAllister helped me as I slithered out of the saddle. She made me sit on some straw bales with my head between my knees.

"Did you skip breakfast, Lyndsey?" I heard her ask.

I thought about my squashed Weetabix. Not much of it had made it into my mouth. "Kind of," I said to the floor.

"That'll be it then," said Mrs McAllister firmly. "Nothing to worry about. Just nerves and excitement on an empty tummy. Here..." I heard a rustle and then felt something pushed into my hand. It was a cereal bar.

"Have a munch on that," said Mrs McA, "and we'll try again in ten minutes."

"Can I come back another day instead?" I looked up, but she was already striding back to her office.

"I don't think that would be a good idea," she called over her shoulder. "If you give in to nerves today, tomorrow you'll feel worse. I'll be back in ten minutes!"

That afternoon the other Sleepover girls were due to pile round to mine for a big session painting the cardboard cut-outs for the presentation. I'd been looking forward to it. But now I didn't want to see anyone, and I didn't want to do anything. I felt like a cuddly toy that's lost its stuffing.

"Buck up," said Mum. "Your friends'll be here in a minute."

When the doorbell rang it was all I could do to stretch my face into a smile.

"Hey, Fliss, are you moving in?" laughed my dad when he saw her lugging an enormous holdall into our sitting room.

"I haven't brought that much," she said to

me. "Just a few costume options." My efforts to look normal clearly weren't working that well, because the next second she looked at me narrowly and said, "Hey, Lyndz, is something wrong?"

"Yes," I said flatly. "I—"

But before I could tell her what had happened, the doorbell rang again.

Frankie and Kenny were standing on the doorstep, attacking each other with paintbrushes. "See – we brought our own!" squealed Frankie, as Kenny tried to 'paint' her ear. They lurched past me, still grappling with one another, just as Rosie's car drew up.

"Mum's on her way to take Adam to his riding lesson," Rosie said a moment later, waving as the car pulled out of our driveway. (You probably know this already, but Rosie's brother has cerebral palsy, and he goes to the same stables as me. Mrs McAllister's a registered Riding for the Disabled teacher.) As the car disappeared, Rosie turned to me. "So – how'd it go this morning?"

I opened my mouth and shut it again. I felt pathetic. If Adam, with his celebral palsy, was brave enough to sit on a pony, how come I wasn't?

"Dreadful," I said at last. "I just couldn't do it."

"Couldn't do what?" yelled Kenny from the sitting room.

Rosie smiled and led me in. "Nosy Parker," she said to Kenny.

Kenny shrugged. "A problem shared is a problem doubled." She frowned. "Or have I got that wrong?"

"Go on, Lyndz," said Rosie, flopping on the sofa. "What were you saying?"

"This morning," I said. "I just couldn't ride. I tried – twice – and it was no use."

"Why not? Was your arm hurting?"

"No, nothing like that." I hesitated. I could still hardly believe it myself. "I was *scared*. Maybe this'll sound crazy to you, but I've just never thought of riding as dangerous before. Now all of a sudden it terrifies me."

"Oh, I've *always* known riding was dangerous," said Fliss. "Remember that time I was stuck on a runaway horse? I could've been— ouch! What was that for?"

Kenny had kicked her. "Horses give you the heebie-jeebies anyway, Fliss, so you don't count," she said.

Rosie grabbed my hand and pulled me down to sit next to her. "Of course you can get some bumps and bruises riding but, well, you're not exactly going to do something really hard, like ride in the Grand National, are you?"

"Rosie's right," said Frankie. "You were really unlucky, Lyndz, but you're a seriously good rider. And riding's not mega dangerous – not like an extreme sport or something."

"Like that rock climbing Tom Cruise does in *Mission Impossible 2*," said Kenny, her eyes lighting up. "When he dangles off this enormous cliff by one arm! Molly had it out on video," she explained.

"Or that thing they do at the Winter Olympics when people lie on a tea tray and whizz head-first down a chute at a million miles an hour," said Fliss.

"Yeah, that is *so* wicked!" said Frankie. "Hey, Lyndz, you've got to admit it – riding's pretty tame by comparison, isn't it?"

"You're right," I said. "I'm being a wimp. Let's just forget it. I'll be fine."

And in a few moments it was forgotten – except by me.

CHAPTER EIGHT

"Fliss? Don't you want the rest of your crumble?"

Fliss shook her head. "I'm full," she said, pushing the bowl across the table to me. We were in the dining hall at school. It was Thursday, the day before our presentations.

"You're packing it away today, Lyndz," laughed Frankie. "Have your mum and dad stuck you on a diet at home, or something?"

I smiled. "No way! I've got another riding lesson after school today, that's all. And I reckon the problem last time was that I hadn't had enough breakfast. That's why I felt faint."

"Hope the ponies are feeling strong," said Kenny, with a cheeky wink.

I didn't mind the teasing but, to be honest, I wasn't in much of a mood to laugh along. I was too nervous about going to the stables. More than anything else in the world, I wanted to get it right this time. For now, I tried to concentrate on the rest of Fliss's apple crumble and hoped I wouldn't get indigestion.

By the time I got home from school later that afternoon, though, my nerves were worse than ever. "You'll be fine, sweetheart," said Mum, seeing my worried face. "You just need to get back into the swing of it, that's all."

Get back into the swing of it – that sounded about right. But how? When I got to the stables I fetched Bramble's brushes, combs and sponges and groomed her slowly and carefully. "We'll be OK, won't we, Bramble?" I said. Her soft eyes stared back at me, and suddenly I felt much better. How could anything to do with such a lovely, gentle pony be scary?

Later, when I jumped up into her saddle, I really felt almost fine. There were only three or four butterflies flapping in my tummy rather than hundreds. I was so relieved.

But I shouldn't have been. As soon as I put Bramble into a walk, the sick, dizzy feeling came flooding back.

"I can't do this, Mrs McAllister," I said, shaking my head in desperation. "I just can't. I've got to get down."

"Come on, now, Lyndsey," said Mrs McAllister. I could see she was annoyed. "Don't give in to it again, for goodness' sake. Have a bit of courage!"

My stomach was churning, my head was spinning. Leaning forward, I clung to Bramble's neck. "I'm sorry, dear Bramble," I sobbed into her mane. "It's not that I don't want to ride you – you know that, don't you? I just don't know what's wrong with me. I'm *so* sorry..."

The next morning I should've woken up feeling on top of the world. It was the last day of school before half-term – *and* the day we were due to give our presentations. Sometimes I think the last schoolday is even better than the holiday itself, because you've got all that lovely free time still to come. It's like the delicious moment just before you dig in to a big piece of chocolate cake!

This morning, though, you could've given me the most enormous chocolate cake ever baked and I would hardly have smiled. I couldn't remember feeling so miserable before in my entire life.

When I arrived at school, Kenny and Frankie bounded out of the playground to help me and Dad get the cardboard cut-outs from the car.

"Wow! They look sooo cool!" squealed Rosie, who was watching us over the railings and waving Frankie's horse mask.

Soon the bell rang. As our class lined up to go inside, I noticed several people clutching strange-shaped bags and boxes filled with costumes and props. Everyone was whispering excitedly. Even Mrs Weaver looked cheerful.

"Pipe down, now!" she called when we got into the classroom. "The sooner I take the register, the sooner we can get on to the fun!"

Once the register was finished, Mrs Weaver delved into her bag and pulled out two enormous boxes of sweets. There was a huge tub of Roses – "For the team giving the best presentation," explained Mrs Weaver – and a slightly smaller box of Celebrations for the runners-up.

"Prizes – even better!" whispered Kenny with a grin. "The Roses are ours, guys!"

Next Mrs Weaver wrote a running order up on the board – the order the teams were going to perform in. We were second, after Regina Hill's team, who were doing 'Houses and Homes'. So, while Regina and co. were performing, we legged it over to the cloakroom to get our costumes on.

"I'm so nervous!" giggled Rosie, pulling on a tweed waistcoat over her white school shirt. She had a matching cap, too – she'd found them in a charity shop. "You're all right, Kenny – you can hide behind Frankie."

107

"Why d'you think I wanted to be the back end of the horse?" grinned Kenny, who was trying to work out which way to put on her brown tights. We'd made a woollen tail for her and attached it to a belt that she was going to wear over her tights.

"Lyndz, can you do me up?" asked Fliss, backing towards me. A long row of hooks and eyes ran down the back of her dress.

"I'll give it a go," I said.

I was going to be the driver of Fliss's carriage. I didn't have anything really Victorian to wear, but I thought a posh lady's servant should look quite smart, so I'd got a pair of black trousers and a black blazer that my brother Tom had grown out of. They were only a bit too big for me.

By now Frankie, Kenny and Rosie were ready. "We should go back and sort out the props," said Frankie. "You two catch us up, OK?"

"All right," said Fliss, breaking off from muttering her speech under her breath. "Hurry, Lyndz!"

"I'm going as fast as I can," I said. I'm no good with fiddly things if I'm in a hurry, and I kept getting the wrong hook in the wrong eye. At last I was finished.

"You're all done," I said, and flopped down on the bench.

"Come on, Lyndz," Fliss said. "We'll be starting in a sec, and you haven't even got your shoes on."

I didn't want to move. What was the point? I was bound to muck this up, just like I'd mucked up my riding. "You go on without me," I said, flapping a hand towards the door. "I bet Rosie knows my speech, anyway. And I'll only get it wrong. I'm so hopeless."

"You're not!" said Fliss, putting her hands on her hips. "You were brilliant in that run-through the other day!"

I shrugged. "That was before."

"Before what? Lyndz, what is wrong with you today? You're being a right misery-guts!"

And so I told her about my riding lesson. By the time I'd finished I had hot tears dribbling down my cheeks. "I've got about as much chance of riding a horse again as Frankie and Kenny have of turning into one!" I wailed.

Fliss crouched in front of me and took hold of my elbows. "Look, Lyndz. I know you must be really upset. But this presentation's got nothing to do with riding. You can do this standing on your head." She smiled. "It's nearly half-term. We're about to win a monster box of chocolates. A couple of reasons to be cheerful, don't you think?"

"I guess."

Just then Frankie poked her head round the door. "Hey, guys, can you hurry up? They're waiting for us."

Fliss stood up and held out her hands. "We can talk about your riding lesson afterwards," she said, pulling me up. "The Sleepover Club will come to the rescue! We'll think of something, I promise. OK?"

"OK." I took a deep breath and wiped my cheeks. "Let's go."

Our presentation went down a storm, right from the first moment when Rosie climbed on a chair holding the cardboard bicycle. We'd painted legs on the bicycle, wearing trousers that matched her waistcoat, so it looked like she was riding it. Everyone clapped even before she started her speech!

Next, Frankie and Kenny came clip-clopping on as the horse, with me holding the 'reins' (actually brown ribbons) behind them. They looked so hilarious in their costume that the whole class fell about laughing, which was way cool. Behind me came Fliss in her long party dress, holding up the big cardboard picture we'd made of the side of a carriage. She held it in front of her legs so that it looked like she was sitting in the carriage, being pulled along.

I got through my piece about horses OK, though I think I rushed it a bit. Then Fliss and Rosie struck up a conversation about "these new-fangled things called trains" and how fast they went and how dangerous and dirty they were. At this point I had to sneak away and grab the cardboard steam train we'd made and make it chug along at the back, as if it was going past while they talked. When they'd finished, I pressed 'Play' on Mrs Weaver's tape recorder and Frankie and Kenny went into their dance routine as a finale.

At the end the whole class cheered. "I think Laura and Francesca could get a job in a panto in Leicester next Christmas!" laughed Mrs Weaver.

"That was ace!" whispered Frankie, pulling off her horse mask and holding up her hand for high fives as we went back to our seats (we were going to change later so we wouldn't miss any of the other presentations). "It's in the bag, girls!"

But a minute later she didn't look so sure. The M&Ms' group was on next. Their subject was 'Schools' ("Trust them to choose the swottiest topic!" as Kenny had said). The trouble was, it was good. Emily Berryman was a strict schoolmaster, with a swishy cane and the most enormous moustache you can imagine.

"Right, you horrible lot!" she snarled. "I am going to tell you about Victorian schools. And they were not places for having fun!"

Next came the group doing 'Costume', who'd worked out a puppet show as part of their presentation. "Botheration," whispered Kenny behind me. "This one's really good too!"

After that, Ryan Scott's group did 'Sports and Pastimes', and Alana Palmer's group finished up with 'Animals', which would've been OK except that Alana completely forgot her words in the middle and ran out of the classroom, her face bright red. Mrs Weaver had to go and fetch her to make her carry on.

To be honest, when the time came for Mrs Weaver to announce the winners, I don't think any of us were feeling very confident.

"And the first prize goes to..." Mrs Weaver held up the gigantic tub of Roses. "...Emily's team!"

Behind me, I heard Kenny and Frankie groan. The M&Ms, meanwhile, hugged each other as if they were film stars, before going up to nab the chocolates.

"If they scoff that lot they'll turn into the flabbiest spot-monsters ever!" whispered Rosie.

Meanwhile, Mrs Weaver was reaching for the Celebrations. "I am awarding the second prize," she said, "for best entertainment value. And this goes to... Lyndsey's group!"

Well, I did grin then, for the first time that day. Frankie went to fetch our prize, but when she came back she plonked the box on my desk. "Result!" she said, beaming at me.

"What d'you reckon 'best entertainment value' means?" asked Kenny a few minutes later when we were squashed with all the other girls in the cloakroom, trying to get changed.

"It means that ours was the best laugh," said Rosie.

"And these are by far the best chocolates," said Frankie, dipping her arm into the box for the umpteenth time. "Celebrations beat Roses any day! Yum!"

I was undoing Fliss's hooks and eyes. "Well done, Lyndz," she said over her shoulder. "Are you feeling better?"

"Better about what?" said Kenny. "Are you OK, Lyndz?"

"She had a horrid time at her riding lesson again yesterday," Fliss explained.

"Hmm, bummer," said Kenny sympathetically.

"And I told her the Sleepover Club would come to the rescue," Fliss went on.

"Great idea!" said Frankie. "Don't worry, Lyndz. We'll all help."

"We'll take you in hand!" said Rosie.

"Look, it's dead kind of you," I said, tapping Fliss's shoulder to let her know I'd finished on the hooks and eyes. "But there's nothing you can do. Anyway..." I shrugged. "It really doesn't matter that much. It's no big deal."

The others were quiet, pulling on socks and doing up buttons. I could tell they didn't believe me.

CHAPTER NINE

"Hey, Lyndz!" yelled Tom from the bottom of the stairs. "It's one of your weird friends on the phone!"

It was the next morning – the first morning of half-term – and I was fresh out of the shower. Hugging my towel around me, I stumped down the stairs, sticking out my tongue at Tom as I passed him.

"Lyndz?" said a familiar voice when I picked up the receiver. "It's Fliss. Look, I know it's short notice, but can you come to a sleepover at mine tonight?"

"I certainly hope so," I said. "I need

116

something to look forward to. Let me just check with Mum."

I think Mum was pleased to get the "wet weekend", as she called me, off her hands. At any rate, she said I could go, and soon I was stuffing my overnight things into my bag and raiding the kitchen cupboard for any stray biscuits or crisps. Usually we make a bit of an effort with what we wear to sleepovers, but today, standing in front of my wardrobe, I just couldn't get enthusiastic about anything. Eventually I grabbed a yellow T-shirt and sweatshirt, and my oldest, softest pair of jeans.

When Fliss opened her front door a few hours later I could tell she hadn't had the same problem. She was wearing a pair of smart pink trousers I hadn't seen before, and a pink spangly top. I was dreading her saying something disapproving about my jeans, but she just grinned and ushered me inside, saying, "Wait till you hear, Lyndz! I've had *the* fabbest idea!"

In the sitting room I found Britney Spears going full blast on the CD player. Kenny was wailing along, doing all the actions from the new video, while Rosie and Frankie fell about laughing.

"What's your idea, then?" I shouted at Fliss above the din.

"Hang on." She went and turned the music down, to howls of protest from Kenny. Then, while the rest of us flopped on the floor, she grabbed a glossy magazine from the coffee table and flicked through it. The magazine was called *Perfect Homes, Perfect Lives* – the sort of thing that tells you how to decorate your home, as long as your home is an enormous mansion and you have pots of money.

Fliss found the right page and spread it open on the carpet.

"Look!" she said, pointing to a big advert that took up a whole page. "The Wentworth Equestrian Show."

"What's 'equestrian', when it's at home?" asked Kenny, peering at the picture, which showed a man on a horse sailing over a big jump.

"It means to do with horse-riding," I said.

118

Fliss tapped the page. "It's this coming Friday," she said. "And I reckon we should all go. Club outing. To help you get your confidence back."

I looked round at the others. Fliss must've told them about it before I arrived, because they were all grinning at me expectantly. "Er... that's a really kind thought, Fliss," I said. "But you'd hate it, you know. There'd be horses everywhere."

"I realise that," said Fliss primly. Then she smiled. "I think it'll be a laugh. And Mum has said she can take us. Andy's got the day off work, so he can look after the twins. It's all arranged."

"Wow." I didn't really know what to say. "Are you sure, guys? I'll feel so guilty if you're just going for me."

"Are you kidding?" Kenny pointed at the magazine picture. "Fliss is going for those Brad Pitts on horseback, I guarantee it."

"Don't be stupid!" said Fliss. But she turned pink as she said it, which gave the rest of us a major fit of the giggles.

* * *

119

The Wentworth Equestrian Show was being held in the Wentworth Arena, a big indoor sports stadium near Birmingham. Nikki, Fliss's mum, drove us there in her new 'people carrier', which was kind of like a cross between a car and a mini-bus. It was dead swanky.

"It's not going to be posh, this show, is it?" said Rosie, as we pulled into a service station for some petrol. "You don't think we should've dressed up?" We were all wearing jeans and trainers.

"It's horse racing people dress up for," said Fliss. "Like Ascot and stuff. Isn't that right, Lyndz?"

"I think so," I said. "No one looks smart at our stables, anyhow. It's far too muddy."

The Arena turned out to be massive, with lots of different entrances and exits, and it took us ages to find the door that was marked on our tickets.

"Hey, they do pop concerts here!" said Frankie, looking at some posters as we queued to get in. "We should come and see Gareth Gates sometime!"

"Nooo, Will Young!" chorused Fliss and Rosie.

"Not so loud, you'll give me a headache," said Nikki, frowning. "And keep together, girls. I don't want to lose anyone."

When we finally got to our seats we found we were quite high up, so we had a really good view. The programme said there was going to be a junior 'show' class and a junior jumping competition, and then later on there'd be adult show jumping.

"I want to see someone go splosh in the water," said Kenny, reading the programme over my shoulder. "I remember seeing it on the telly once: the horse stopped in front of the jump and just tipped its rider in. It was *so* funny!"

I shivered. Even the *idea* of falling off gave me the wobbles these days. But I just said, "You only get water-jumps on cross-country courses. Not indoors."

"Oh, swizz," said Kenny cheerfully.

When the junior show class started, I could tell Kenny was a bit bored. "So... what's the point of this bit?" she whispered to me. "Are they going to *do* something soon?"

I didn't get a chance to answer. To my amazement, Fliss jumped in. "What do you mean, what's the point?" she hissed. "Have you seen the totally brilliant way number 51's done her hair? Look, the ribbon weaves right through her plait, it's so cool... Hey, Lyndz – can you do that for me when we get home?"

"Um, I can try," I said.

Kenny was happier when the jumping competition started – probably because she was hoping someone would fall off.

"I'm sticking up for number 24," declared Frankie. "She looks like me."

Number 24 was a girl with dark hair. You couldn't tell much else as we were sitting so high up.

But there was no stopping Frankie. When the girl finished her round she jumped to her feet and yelled, "Yeah! We love you, 24!"

"Oh no," muttered Fliss into her programme. "We're not with her, OK?"

I giggled. I was really chuffed my friends were having fun – I'd been worried that they'd hate it and I'd get the blame.

When the junior jumping was finished (the dark-haired girl didn't win a prize, much to Frankie's disgust) there was a long interval while they set up the big jumps for the grown-ups, so we headed off to find some food.

"Keep together, girls, won't you?" said Nikki, who was staying with our coats (Fliss told us afterwards she was on a diet). "And be back here by..."She looked at her smart gold wristwatch. "...say, three o'clock?"

This gave us more than half an hour to explore the stalls selling food and clothes and magazines that'd been set up outside the main arena. Frankie and Fliss wanted to try on everything from ranger's hats to stripy wellies and waxed jackets, but Kenny insisted on food first. I was glad, because my tummy was rumbling. We found a booth selling hot baked potatoes and sat down on some ornamental straw bales to eat them.

"Well..." said Frankie, with a mouth half full of potato and grated cheese, "what's it feel like, Lyndz? Knowing that one day we'll be here watching *you*?"

"Hey, yeah!" said Rosie. "That would be amazing! We'd cheer you over every jump!"

I smiled and shook my head. "Won't happen," I said.

"Seriously, though," said Rosie, "how're you feeling, Lyndz?"

"Is it working, do you think?" asked Fliss. "Are you feeling any better?"

Kenny nudged me. "You must admit – it's pretty fab, right? Even I think so and I'm not into all this horsey stuff."

I knew my friends were trying hard – I knew it was for my sake, too. But I just couldn't bear any more. I said, "No, it's not fab! I mean, today's wonderful, and I'm really glad I came, but..." I stared down into my baked potato, feeling all their eyes on me. "... but please stop asking if I feel better. I just don't. And I won't."

"Come on," said Rosie. "Don't give up so easily."

"I've tried my best!" I shouted, raising my head at last. "I'm never going to ride again and that's that. Do you understand? Finished!" I stuffed my polystyrene potato carton into the overflowing bin next to me and stood up. "Now can we just forget it and enjoy the rest of the show?"

The journey back in the car was pretty miz. Nikki knew something was wrong – I guess she just thought we'd had a quarrel. She kept chirping on brightly about what an interesting day it'd been, as if she wanted us to start chatting about it. No one did.

Because I live outside Cuddington, I was the first to be dropped off. The others all got out and gave me a hug, which was dead sweet of them considering how grumpy I'd been. "I'll ring you tomorrow," I said to Rosie, who was the last to get back into the car.

"You'd better," she said, and grinned.

When I got in I went straight to my room and flung myself down on my bed. In a way, going to the Wentworth Show had made it all worse. It had brought home to me how much had changed. A few weeks ago I would have been so excited, sitting at the show thinking,

"I'm going to do that one day." Today, watching those gorgeous horses had just made me feel like a wimp and a failure.

I sat up, and looked round at my horse posters on the walls, and the pile of pony magazines by my bed. Even they had changed. My favourite belongings had become horrible reminders of what I couldn't do any more. I felt like tearing them into tiny shreds.

But I didn't. One by one, carefully, I took my posters down and folded them on top of the magazines. Then I pushed the whole lot deep into the dusty shadows under my bed. Burying my face in the duvet, I burst into tears.

The next morning, as promised, I rang Rosie. "I'm so sorry about yesterday," I said. "I hope I didn't spoil it for everyone else."

"You didn't spoil it," said Rosie. "We were worried about you, that's all. How – er..." She hesitated.

"How am I?" I said, almost laughing. "You're allowed to ask, you know! I'm OK. Much better."

"That's brilliant!" She sounded really relieved.

"Listen, I'm going to the stables this afternoon," I said, "and I wondered if you'd mind coming too? I want to give back the riding hat Mrs McAllister lent me yonks ago. And..." Now it was my turn to hesitate. "...and I want to say goodbye to the ponies."

"Say goodbye?" said Rosie, sounding concerned again. "But you can carry on seeing them, can't you? Lyndz, you know how much you love Bramble and the others!"

I was not going to cry. I was *not*. I swallowed hard and said, "Yes, I know. But if I can't ride, going there will just make me feel sad. The ponies have lots of other people to love them and take care of them. They won't miss me."

"I bet they will—" began Rosie. But then she stopped herself and said, "Of course we'll go with you. All of us. I'll ring the others. The Sleepover Club sticks together through thick and thin!"

I was glad Rosie had said yes. If she and

the others were with me, I'd have to hold myself together.

They turned up straight after lunch, Frankie and Kenny in one car, and Rosie and Fliss in another.

"I've persuaded Mum and Dad that we should have a big slap-up tea when we get back," I said, showing off the carrier bag full of mini-rolls, muffins and Battenburg cake (my favourite!) that Dad had just lugged back from the supermarket.

"Lip-smackin' good!" said Kenny in her best cowgirl voice. "Can we have a little something for the road?"

"No, you can't!" laughed Dad, snatching the bag from me in the nick of time. "I'll see you later, gang. Now, shoo!"

We walked to the stables, which didn't take long. As we turned the corner into the lane, I could see that Bramble was on her own in one of Mr Brocklehurst's fields.

"Do you want me to run and ask Mrs McAllister for the padlock key?" asked Rosie. She knew that the gates to all the fields are kept firmly locked.

I shook my head. "It's a combination lock, this one," I said, "and I know the number off by heart."

"Go on, then," said Rosie softly. "We'll wait for you in the yard."

So, while my friends headed on towards the stable buildings, I trudged over to the gate, and a minute later I was in the field.

Bramble lifted her head and came trotting to meet me. I'd brought some pony nuts, so I fished them out of my pocket.

"Hey, Bramble," I said, holding out my hand for her. When she'd finished eating, I laid my cheek against her neck, drinking in the familiar smell of her beautiful clean coat. I felt hot tears trickle down my nose. Bramble stood there patiently, as if she understood.

"It isn't that I don't love you – you know that, huh?" I whispered, stroking her, over and over. "You're the best pony in the world, Bramble. And I've loved riding you. I just... can't do it any more." I lifted my head to see the kind brown eyes looking at me softly. "Other people will love you now," I said. I kissed her nose. "Goodbye."

By the time I got to the gate I could hardly see a thing. But I sniffed hard and swallowed back my tears, rubbing my sleeve roughly across my cheeks.

I heard gales of laughter coming from the yard. Trojan was standing tethered outside his stall, all tacked up and ready for a riding lesson. Lisa Bentham was standing beside him, trying to teach Fliss how to feed him a piece of carrot.

"Aiiieee! It tickles!" Fliss squealed, turning her head away and jigging from foot to foot, while Kenny, Frankie and Rosie collapsed in fits of giggles.

"Keep still, will you!" laughed Lisa. "You'll spook him!"

It made me smile, too. But when the others saw me, their laughter faded.

"Can you watch Trojan for a moment, Lyndsey?" asked Lisa. "I need to have a word with Miranda."

"No problem," I said.

"Poor Lyndz!" said Frankie, rushing over as soon as Lisa had gone.

"No, I'm OK," I insisted, shrugging her off.

"Really. Thanks, Frankie." The sight of my friends' faces had made me realise what a downer I was putting on all our lives these days. "You know what, guys?" I said, giving Trojan a brisk pat and smiling round at them. "No more misery-guts Lyndz! I'm fed up with being gloomy and I'm pretty sure you must be, too. You don't need to tiptoe round me any more. We're the Sleepover Club! We should be having fun!"

"Too right!" said Frankie. "Yee-hah!"

"Now – I'll just go and find Mrs McAllister and give her this," I said, waving my riding hat. "And then it's back to mine for a nosh-up!"

Rosie and Frankie cheered. Fliss was still wiping Trojan's dribble off her hand. Kenny, meanwhile, was staring at something in the distance. "Hey," she said, pointing towards Mr Brocklehurst's field. "Is that pony allowed out?"

I turned my head. And stared. The gate of Bramble's field was standing open. And there was Bramble, tail held high in excitement, trotting off down the lane that led out of the stables towards the road.

"But how—" I began. I was sure I'd fastened the gate as I left the field.

The next moment, an image flashed into my mind of Bramble trotting down the middle of the main road, while just round the bend, a car speeds towards her at sixty miles an hour, unable to see her, too late to brake...

"Noooo!" I screamed, setting off after her as fast as I could. "Bramble! Come back!"

But after a few steps I stopped. There was no way I could catch her. Desperate, I raced back to the yard. I thought of running to the office to tell Mrs McAllister, but every minute wasted was a minute longer that Bramble would be on the road, and in danger.

In that instant, I made a decision.

"Fliss! Untie Trojan's reins!" I commanded. "Quick!"

Fumbling frantically, Fliss did as she was told. I jammed the riding hat I was still carrying on to my head and fastened the strap. Then I grabbed Trojan's reins and put my hands on his back.

"Frankie, can you give me a leg-up?"

"Sure thing..."

A moment later I was in the saddle.

"Has she reached the end of the lane yet?" I said to the others. "Can you see which way she's turning?"

"Uh, I can't – oh, yes – she's turning right," said Rosie, who'd climbed on to the gate at the yard entrance to get a better view.

"OK," I said, thinking quickly. "If I head across the fields I can try to cut her off at the bend in the road by the next village." I squeezed my legs and directed Trojan towards the open gate. "Tell Mrs McAllister!" I yelled over my shoulder, as I pushed Trojan into a gallop.

I was vaguely aware of Frankie, Kenny and Fliss in a huddle in the yard, clutching one another in anxiety.

"Good luck, Lyndz!" I heard Kenny yell behind me.

And then I had to turn every ounce of my attention to Trojan. We were going to have to ride like the wind across Mr Brocklehurst's farm. There were several fences between us and the far road, and with no time to lose there was only one thing we could do: jump them.

CHAPTER TEN

Later – much later – Rosie told me that Mrs McAllister had been furious when she'd found out what had happened.

"She was like a whole box of fireworks going off at once!" she said, her eyes wide at the memory. "She was tearing around, grabbing the collar and rope and her car keys, and all the time she kept shouting about who on earth could be stupid enough not to shut a gate, and about what she'd do when she got her hands on them. We were really scared she was going to beat you up or something!"

I was kind of glad I hadn't been there at the time. Where I *was*, I had no chance to bother about Mrs McAllister or anyone else.

Trojan was going at a cracking pace, faster than I'd ever ridden before in my life. He seemed to know it was an emergency, and that we were going to have to do some crazy things.

We got to the far side of Bramble's field in no time. But here the fence was just too high and I had to rein Trojan in. Growling with frustration I turned him, and we headed off along the fence, looking for a way round or through.

At the north end of the field, the fence gave way to a hedge. It was fairly high, and I didn't fancy trying it, but I couldn't see any option.

"Come on, Trojan, we can do this," I said, urging him on, letting him know that I was determined to jump, that I was confident.

It's too high – it's got to be too high, I thought as we drew nearer to the hedge. But we had to get to Bramble. I kept picturing her and that speeding car... Already we could be too late.

The next moment Trojan pushed off, his powerful hind legs underneath him. I leant forward, back straight, keeping my hands as light on the reins as I could manage.

Trojan powered through the air, his neck stretched forward. Then his forelegs uncurled to touch the ground. We'd done it – we had reached the other side!

I almost laughed with relief. But we weren't done yet. We had to jump three more fences before we reached the village. Luckily, none of them were as high as the first hedge, and Trojan sailed over them like an old pro.

The village, Milton Hamlet, is like something on a holiday postcard, with rows of cottages and neat little gardens. What I must've looked like, clattering up the high street all flushed and anxious on a sweating pony, I've no idea – I probably spoiled the view!

I passed the church and the village shop, and caught sight of a woman in a blue body-warmer whom I'd seen at the stables once or twice, though I didn't know her name. And there, not far from her, stood Bramble, snorting and frightened, but unscathed.

"Have you come looking for this one?" asked the woman. "She seems to know you."

It was true. Bramble had stopped pacing and was staring at Trojan and me.

"She escaped from McAllister's stables," I said.

"Let's get her off the road," said the woman. "My front garden will do as a pen." She pointed to a nearby cottage.

Hastily, I dismounted, and led Trojan towards Bramble. Then, using Trojan and me as a kind of 'guide fence' to stop Bramble from bolting back along the road, the woman managed to herd her into the little garden.

"Phew! Talk about a relief!" said the woman. "How on earth did she get out?"

"I don't know," I said. "I was sure I'd shut the gate, but…"

My voice trailed off when I saw the severe look on the woman's face. Then her expression softened and she said, "You won't make that mistake again, I expect. I take it you knew what danger she was in?"

"Too right," I said. I could hardly bear to think about it.

At that moment Mrs McAllister's Land Rover roared into view. Seeing us, she pulled over to the side of the road and stopped the engine. I saw her sit for a minute staring at Bramble. It wasn't until then that I realised how funny Bramble looked – standing with her head poking out over the garden gate, framed by a beautiful arch of creepers, as if she was just watching the world go by.

Mrs McAllister was still gripping the steering wheel. I saw her rest her forehead on her hands for a moment. Then she collected herself and got out, striding across to the woman in the blue body-warmer.

"Sandra," said Mrs McAllister, "I really can't thank you enough. I don't know how this happened..."

"Thank goodness I spotted her," said Sandra, giving Bramble's neck an affectionate pat.

"And Lyndsey..." Mrs McAllister turned to me. "I must congratulate you on your quick thinking. And on your riding skills, young lady!"

Do you know what? I looked at Mrs McAllister... I looked at Trojan. And it was only then that it hit me what I'd done. I'd been sitting in that saddle. I'd got all the way from the stables to Milton Hamlet on a pony, and I'd even had to jump fences to do it!

"You've found your confidence again, I suspect?" said Mrs McAllister with a smile.

I grinned back. "Bramble found it for me."

We both looked at my favourite pony. "We should get you home," said Mrs McA, stroking Bramble's nose.

Mrs McAllister went to the Land Rover and got out a headcollar and a lead rope. With Sandra's help, she fastened the collar in place and attached the lead rope's clip.

"Now, Lyndsey," she said, turning to me. "Do you think you might be able to ride Trojan back to the stables, leading Bramble? If you're at all unsure, I could drive back and fetch Lisa."

"No, I'll be fine," I said firmly.

Riding on a road and leading another

pony is not the easiest thing in the world but luckily I didn't meet many cars – and those that did come along slowed right down as they passed. Bramble was as good as gold, and Trojan was on his best behaviour too.

When we turned into the lane that leads to the stables, a massive whoop went up, and I saw Rosie, Kenny, Frankie and Fliss bouncing up and down and waving frantically.

"You did it!" they squealed when I reached the yard.

I handed Bramble's lead rope to Miranda, then dismounted and gave Lisa Trojan's reins. "I'm sorry I borrowed him," I said.

"That's quite all right," Lisa grinned. "I'm glad he made himself useful!"

Then my friends fell on me for a major group hug.

"Hey – Bramble had to resort to pretty desperate measures to get you riding again, didn't she?" said Frankie.

"It's a total mystery how it happened," said Rosie. "I definitely saw you put the latch down as you came out of the field – I remember it really clearly, because I was worried about how upset you were."

There's a metal latch on the field gate that raises and lowers. Intelligent ponies like Bramble soon learn how to nudge it up with their noses, though. That's why you need a padlock too.

"I must've forgotten to put the padlock on," I said. "How stupid!"

"So it was *you*!"

I spun round. I hadn't realised Mrs McAllister had got out of her Land Rover and was standing just behind me.

"Stupid is just the start of it," she snapped, slamming the door shut. "How about reckless, irresponsible..." Suddenly she stopped, and let out a big sigh. "You know what could've happened. You must've been just as worried as me, Lyndsey, or you wouldn't have shot off on Trojan like that. And I expect whatever you went through was punishment enough, eh?"

I nodded, biting my lip.

"Remind me, though," said Mrs McAllister, "I must have a word with Mr Brocklehurst.

He'll need to be assured my pupils aren't going to make a habit of careering across his fields with no warning."

I undid the strap on my riding hat and pulled it off. "I'd come today to return this," I said to Mrs McAllister, "and to tell you that I was giving up riding."

"Oh, Lyndsey—"

"Don't worry," I broke in quickly. "I reckon I may have changed my mind."

"Well, I won't say it was all worthwhile, because putting Bramble's life in danger was unforgivable," said Mrs McA. "But at least something good has come out of it, hey?" She tapped my hat. "You'd like to hang on to this for a bit longer, I hope?"

"If that's OK," I said, and grinned.

When Mrs McAllister had gone back into her office, Rosie, Kenny, Frankie and Fliss clustered round me again.

"How did it feel?" asked Rosie. "I couldn't believe it when you just jumped on Trojan right there and then and whizzed off. It was like something in a film!"

"You know what? It felt like the most

natural thing in the world." I shook my head, still hardly able to believe it. "Whatever the problem was before, it seems to have broken the jinx. I think everything's going to be OK from here on."

"As long as you remember to shut the gate!" laughed Kenny.

Can you imagine how much I've been teased about that since? I'll never live it down, I reckon! It's great to be able to laugh about something so scary, though – I think it stops me having nightmares about it.

Oh, blimey, look at us – still sitting here yakking, when Rosie's brother must've finished his riding lesson ages ago. See – there's Rosie's mum's car turning into the yard now. She's come to pick him up.

"Rosie! Tell your mum we don't need a lift! We can walk!"

Did she hear me, d'you reckon? Oh yes, she's waving. There's a sleepover tonight, you see – hosted by yours truly. That's why we've all been hanging out at the stables this afternoon. We're heading back to mine in a minute – Dad's done one of his major cake raids on the supermarket again (sometimes he is way cool!). So I'd better dash or my brothers'll scoff the lot before we get there. Catch you later!